Galactic Mandate

The Scream

By M.R. Richardson

M.R. Richardson

Acknowledgment

I like to thank my beautiful girlfriend Jodi for being the only beta reader. Her input during this process was essential to making my dream become a reality. Thank you to everyone I have met along the way who have given me advice and so much useful information. I could not have done this without the support of my convention friends, professional authors, close friends, and family.

M.R. Richardson

Table of Contents

Chapter 1

Mato was a strapping young man. He didn't remember much more than the reservation. He sat in a wooden boat watching the ocean around them. Nothing stood out, not much to see besides more water. He hated it; he hated it for its beauty and boredom. It moved in endless waves of nothingness.

Handling his spear, he stood up now with the other young men his age. They looked around at each other in their makeshift goggles and snorkels, wearing random scraps of leather and any waterproof material they could find. The sun shone in his eyes, interfering with his ability to see over the side of the boat. The other men, the clones, for they all looked exactly like him, started to dive. This was the task created for his model. This was the way they contributed to the community waiting for them on the shore.

Mato listened for the signal, a long whistle, and yelp that would tell them when to dive with their spears in hand. They would capture a whale that day, enough food to last for weeks, which would be nice. There wasn't always enough food to go around. The reservation was sparsely populated and located on an artificial island. Not much grew on the shore; it was just sand and rocky caves that they took to hiding in when the rains came.

It was time. Eyota blew the whistle, and they were off. Eyota stood out like a sore thumb. He looked nothing like the ragged boys he called brothers. Eyota tried to dress down. He tried to wear tattered clothes that came in natural tones, but everyone could tell the difference. The materials were not the same. They were too new for any clone to afford. The wear patterns were fake and stylized, Mato didn't think Eyota knew any better. The clothes made him believe that this is what he would look like if he were rich and tried to look poor. *I would look silly, that's what I would I look like.*

I shouldn't think such ill will towards Eyota. He is one of the only reasons their home existed. His money personally flowed through the reservation like a river giving it life. Eyota stayed on the boat steering and driving it as the young men jumped off.

The light shinned reflecting off the water blinding Mato for a split second just enough to offset his dive. He stumbled and knocked his head on the side of the boat, sending a quick stream of blood down his face. The other boys who were after him were concerned, and they started to sound a simple alarm. His brothers leaped to his aide.

The others dove down, looking deep into the sea. The clones who had makeshift scuba gear dove down deeper than the rest. They reported back with their hands, making signals up as they went, moving their hands in basic patterns while they swam. The whale they thought they were fishing for started to swim towards them in a strange, illogical way. Panic spread like a shock wave and grabbed them harder than the cold ocean. The unprepared young men speared underneath the waves. They stabbed at the darkness. The large harsh eyes that stared back at them was no whale. It was something new, a monster that they had never encountered before.

The panicked clones tried to swim for the surface, tried anything to get themselves above the water and away from this beast of the sea. It seemed to laugh at their flailing and inept attempts to swim away. The young had taken the wrong bait today. What looked like one known giant monster of the sea was not that at all. Soon the singular set of eyes that they saw became many. What they were looking at was a school of great chameleon sharks. They swarmed the spear fishermen and ate at their bodies. Blood filled the water around them. The ocean turned from deep blue to a maroon of blood, and severed clone body parts floated without their owners.

Mato had been unconscious as his rescuers swum with him away from the massacre. His rescuers looked back in horror as their friends jumped in, not knowing the full scale of the danger that lurked below. More and more clones abandoned the boat to try and save their friends. This only fed the sharks more. Mato started to wake, he stirred his hands and feet suddenly, and his rescuers let him take more control of his own swimming. He awoke to a sight he had trouble comprehending blood in the water and some kind of danger below that he couldn't see. The rescuers panicked, and Eyota, the sole benefactor of one of the last clone reservations, was left the sole occupant of their boat. This was no longer a fishing expedition. Mato swam towards the danger.

"Don't go that way you fool!" his clone brothers shouted.

Mato pointed at the terrified man. "If Eyota dies, we all starve."

"He's about to jump into the water. He is as good as dead over there," they replied. *I can't let that happen.*

He swam towards the danger, leaving his brothers to slow the pace of their retreat and look at each other.

"How is he so fearless?" one of his brothers asked.

"We are the same as him," another said.

"We can do anything he can."

Turning, his brothers followed Mato into danger. They shoved their fear of sharks to the side. The ball of terrifying dread sat in their stomachs as they swam towards the boat.

They swam with urgency, feeling the cold waters against their mostly unprotected skin, slapping it hard with what was turning into a limited supply of energy. They could see Eyota in a daze as he walked towards the edge of the boat.

"Don't jump in," They all yelled separately and desperately. Mato flailed his arms as a warning to not jump in. Fear and panic spread across his face as Eyota misinterpreted this as an invitation to jump to safety. The other young clone men tried to swim even faster as they couldn't let that happen. With the way, the galaxy was today if Eyota was gone their whole race might not make it. The vessel bobbed in the water, and the men looked around to see if they could make the extra twenty-five feet to the boat.

Eyota jumped in. They were too late. The fins of a shark, still hungry from snacking on one of their brothers, swam towards Eyota. Mato had to act fast. *I have to stop this, but how? There is no time to waste.* He saw his brother slightly ahead of him by only a couple of seconds, and they would be next to Eyota, but then what? *What could I do to change what's going to happen?* Mato touched his head noticing the cut that he'd sustained. *That's it, time for action.*

Mato rubbed his face and dove down, spreading the scent of his blood in the water for the sharks to smell. He looked up at the floating carnage. Body parts freely floated above him. He grabbed at them quickly, wielding a severed arm and leg like mallets made of flesh. He waved them around, mixing all the blood with the ocean. This got the shark's attention. It turned towards Mato and ignored Eyota and his other clone brothers who rushed to save the rich man. The shark's eyes locked on Mato, giving the boy its full attention. The shark began to accelerate to full speed.

Mato watched as the clones pushed Eyota back and struggled to get back to the boat.

The shark moved closer. Mato ferociously whacked it in the face again and again with his makeshift weapons, knocking the shark off course. It circled around, giving Mato a chance to look at how Eyota and his brothers were doing. He didn't have any strength left for the shock of seeing two more sharks swimming directly at his brothers. As the shark came at him again, he dropped the arm and leg he'd been using and rolled up onto its back. Using it as a springboard, he jumped towards the boat. Flinging himself over the last couple of yards, he made it back on board. Coming back up onto his feet, he picked up a spear and jabbed into the ocean.

Distressed, he realized that Eyota was the only one left to save. His brothers had been dragged under the ocean leaving him to rage at the water.

"Help me," Eyota cried out.

Mato lent his hand and helped the man up onto the boat.

"This is not what I wanted. I couldn't have known," Eyota muttered.

Mato stabbed again at the bloody ocean.

Eyota got his attention. "Do you smell that?"

"Smell what?"

Eyota looked around while Mato continued to stab at the water. Mato's heart raced, causing him to scream. All of his emotions mixed and intertwined in his noise. Mato himself couldn't tell what the intention of the sounds was. Was it a deep laugh? A heartfelt cry? He just threw the spear back on the deck of the boat while the sharks feasted on his brothers, making odd splashing sounds. Mato fell to knees and he noticed the ocean. He watched the fins circle the boat and pull body parts below the water.

"Fire," Eyota yelled.

Mato stood, turning to look at the smoke that rose from the lower level.

"Don't just sit there grab a bucket," Eyota ordered.

"A bucket?"

"Yes, we need to put this out, or we're going back into the ocean with those monsters!"

"Maybe we should," said Mato. "Maybe this is our fate."

"Don't get melodramatic on me now. We need to save ourselves then figure out what fate has to say about it later." Eyota grabbed a bucket and fearlessly dipped it into the water catching some blood and clone body parts with it. He didn't have time to filter the recent carnage from it. He just grabbed the bucket and ran towards the hatches on the deck of the ship, throwing a stream onto the fire.

Come on boy, it's now or never. What happened to that unyielding spirit from a couple of minutes ago? Don't tell me that you can't lift a bucket after what I just saw. Mato got up and grabbed the nearest bucket. Still seeing the fins of the sharks circling he looked down over the edge of the boat. He turned his head away and refused to look at what he scooped up. Afraid it could be pieces of flesh identical to his own, and to see the red tint of his brothers' blood. *I have to do this. There is no other way.* He tried to clear his mind while he lifted the water and threw it towards fire on the lower level of the boat. Eyota did the same. One man rushed in with water while the other filled a bucket. They were careful not to get into each other's way. The smoke started to get back burning their eyes each time they went back into the boat. They shoveled bucket after bucket onto burning wood until the flames went out. Smoke and steam filled the air around them; a small cloud of haze followed the boat staying just above it while it floated on the ocean.

"Thank you. I'm glad you snapped out of it," Eyota stated.

"I didn't do this for you," Mato replied

"I know son."

"I'm not your son. I'm no one's son. I am only a brother."

"Never thought of it like that. It's certainly true, and you have plenty more back home."

"They are the reason why I saved you."

Eyota raised his finger to point at Mato. "You don't have to be so blatant."

"I don't know of any other way."

"Time will teach you."

The two men seemed to lose interest in talking at the same time. They went back to trying to breathe while the dissipating smoke still filled their lungs. Tired and emotionally drained, they lay on the hard floor of the boat's deck while it rocked to the waves of the ocean. It was quiet again, no other sounds besides the waves and the rocking of the boat. It was somehow so tranquil, shockingly so after what had transpired only moments before.

Mato lay on his back and looked at the stars. He could see the lights of spaceships orbiting the planet as they streaked across the sky. He could see the uncountable number of little white dots in the black sky. The light from them and from the planet's two moons lit up the ocean and the boat in a subtle glow. It was beautiful and awkward to gaze at. Mato wished his brothers could see this again, instead of being sacrificed for a rich man's fishing trip. Eyota fell asleep sitting, hunched over by the interior door. It seemed he did not trust that the fire was gone entirely. Soon Mato's eyes weighed heavy, and he was asleep before he even noticed the change.

A bright spotlight shone in Mato's face from the airship as it hovered above them. Its engines were loud and booming, interrupting the quiet. A downward wind from the ship pressed against Mato. He covered his eyes in an attempt to adjust to his sudden awakening. He realized all the smoke had gone away, and they could be clearly seen. Eyota was waving at the airship, moving his hands from side to side. It turned, revealing a large bay door that opened. It was then Mato that saw more of his cloned brothers. They must have been out searching for them because the boat could no longer check-in. The clones dropped a rope ladder to Mato and Eyota so they could pull themselves up to the airship.

Mato had no problem climbing to join his clone brothers in the airship. He was greeted by all of his brothers who clapped and hollered once he was among them. Eyota struggled to pull himself up the rough and scratchy rope, so Mato's brothers hauled the rope ladder back into the airship dragging Eyota along. They all sighed in relief once Eyota was secured. Marco, one of the most renowned clones in their reservation smacked the side of the ship signaling the captain that it was time to head back.

"We are glad you are back, Eyota. We need your help. The rain has almost started," said Marco

"This early? It's getting to be more frequent," said Eyota

"That is not all. We have visitors who are looking for ya."

"What type of visitors?" he asked

"Soldiers or maybe mercenaries. I'm not sure how to tell the difference."

"Interesting. Must not be too bad. They would have already wrecked the place if it was."

Marco and Mato shared a look of concern. The engines thundered as they started back to the reservation.

"Don't worry, the reservation has nothing to be concerned about," Eyota stated.

The airship flew over the ocean, its spotlights shining on the blue waters. The doors remained open creating a breeze the chilled Mato. He clutched his seat in the airship and brought his knees to his chest while he thought about his return. He thought about the tent he lived in and how it would be empty now. This made him sad.

They reached and saw the shore of the dry, sandy island that they'd come to call home. They watched as the sand gave way to small farms and a rocky desert plain. Further on, this led its way into canyons and caves. They lived on the plains, past the old run-down casinos. Mato could see the long cords of power lines that ran from the towers into the land and back out again. The illegal siphoning kept his people alive. Mato thought about how the casinos with their large neon signs and robotic repair equipment didn't need the power anymore. They'd had their time. No one visited them anymore, and lucky for them. A visitor would complain about the wires which sometimes sparked and burned themselves out. His brothers were always out at the casinos repairing a siphon or starting a new one. It was dangerous work, for sometimes the security system of the old casinos would turn back on, firing lasers at anyone who dared mess with the old buildings. It was so hazardous Mato thought that instead he would take the easier job of fishing. That just didn't work out. His luck   wasn't   so   good.

The airship flew closer to the reservation, and Mato could see the wires reach a point and spread out to cover the walls of a huge gravel pit. It was large enough to fit all the casinos before they were abandoned decades ago. The wires lined the pit, and all the clones could connect to any power line they needed to. It was unreliable but actually quite convenient for what it was. The beige walls of the pits clouded with dust as the airship came to a landing in its designated spot.

The reservation had five airships parked on the flattest area of the cavity. Only two of the five airships worked, the rest were used as luxury houses for the elder clones of the reservation. Eyota looked towards the only permanent structure, his residence, a condo that was carved out of the side of the pit. It had a large panel wall that kept it out of sight from the rest of the reservation. It hid treasures that Mato did not understand. Eyota said he didn't like to rough it for too long in his Condo. Mato had no idea what Eyota considered a real luxury at one of his actual residences. Eyota's place served as a makeshift command center and government administration building for the reservation. When they need to deal with matters off-world the elders came to Eyota and used his equipment.

They landed, and Mato was rushed by the elder clones to the medical tent. He was put on a stretcher and was laid in one of the cots that were what they used as hospital beds. Eyota was escorted back to his condo. He disappeared into it. Mato looked around while in his bed. He enjoyed the rest, of not being on his feet, and the calmness of being back in the place that he knew as home. Even if it was inside the medical tent. The lead nurse came over to examine him. He was no stranger to being hurt, but he hadn't met the head nurse often. Usually one of the other girls his age would help him, or it would be the occasional missionary that came and went. He enjoyed taking pictures with them because sometimes they would let him get a glimpse of the broader galaxy. Mato didn't understand much of what they showed him. They told him about The Acolytes and The Whilom Lytes; they told him the history of the collapse of the CDF. He wondered what it would have been like to be born years ago when the galaxy was at war, and his people rivaled the powers that be instead of hiding and cowering.

The lead nurse bent down. "Are you feeling ok?" she asked.

"Yes, have you heard of me? Give me some drugs, and I will be fine," he replied.

Galactic Mandate: The Scream

"Do you hurt anywhere? All I see is the usual scratches and bruises you late models always have. I heard about what you did. You might have saved all of our asses," said the nurse

"It was nothing. Your model has done way more than we have." He looked at her more closely. "Aren't you a pleasure model?"

She straightened up, her blue eyes lost her warmth, and she grabbed an old beaten down clipboard that was placed by Mato's right side.

"We aren't called pleasure models, we are BCW14s. I know that you know that," she answered.

"Sorry, didn't realize you old lady clones were so sensitive," he replied.

"Old lady? My relative age is 47 cycles," she countered

"Like I said, old lady models," Mato replied. The nurse sneered, pressed intently on her digital board, and moved on.

"You seem fine," she muttered and turned to walk away.

"Hey what about my drugs?" he raised his voice.

"Ask a late model nurse. Oh, wait they don't have access, do they?" she replied.

Mato laid back down and tried to close his eyes. *I can leave in the morning. Nothing beats my own cot, but this will do for tonight.* His eyes narrowed, and he mentally closed the noises of the reservation down until he only heard the sounds of the powerlines. The gentle crackling that was almost omnipresent relaxed him as he went to sleep.

Mato awoke to Eyota staring over him along with some of the elderly models. The lead nurse looked on in the background. "Good morning. I never had a chance to thank you for saving my life. I have been told by our friends outside the planet that the rain is about to start. Your clone elders told me that they want to bestow an honor upon you," Eyota stated.

"When the rain begins, we want you to start the drums. We are giving you the honorary drumstick," an elder stated.

He presents Mato with a large wooden stick with a soft white fur head. Electronic pegs retracted as he handed it over. "Umm, I guess this is an honor, right?" Mato asked.

"Yes, it is. Don't cock it up." Eyota stated as he left.

The elders followed him, but some stopped briefly as they went through the medical tent, saying hello and visiting the sick that weren't contagious. They seem to rush through the other patients as they moved on back to Eyota's residence.

"You see I'm a big deal. Personal friends with Eyota. You better give me the drugs I ask for, or I will tell him myself."

The lead nurse rolled her eyes and walked away. She didn't dignify Mato's request with a response.

A group of nurses looked at him, the later models that were his age.

"Don't play with your stick," one said.

"Ya put that away," from another. They giggled.

Mato looked embarrassed, his cheeks filling up with a rosy glow. Mato got up and moved to vacate the medical tent, but suddenly he felt sore from all the action of the day past. He tried to continue but was stopped when he saw a stretcher with a strange looking person, the likes of which he had never seen before. They were just arriving, and they were going to use the cot he had just left. *Wow, looks like I am already old news.*

"Hey, Mato. Mr. big stick hero man." One of the stretcher bearers --a clone --called to him.

Mato recognized him, the slight differences in their appearance stood out glaringly. It was L2. "What are you talking about?" Mato asked.

"Need some drugs?" L2 replied.

"No, I was only trying to have some fun with the nurses. I'll be fine. I'm not really hurt that bad," Mato said.

"I'm not talking about drugs for your body. I'm talking about drugs for your mind. Some of the best that Natties can offer."

"I don't really mess with that," said Mato.

"Yea, you do. Mr. Big Man. You are literally carrying the biggest stick around, you can have some Derailler. It will derail your mind of troubles."

Mato thought about it for a second. "No, I can't be doing that right now. Like you said, everyone is looking at me now. I'm going to start the rain ceremony, and I want my head clear for that," said Mato.

"Suit yourself, big man. Before long, you will be coming to me," said L2.

Chapter 2

Mato went back to his bunk. He opened his tent to find it stripped of anything useful. Looters had raided it while he had been in the medical tent. The bunk beds were down to just wireframes. Only useless trinkets remained of his and his housemates' possessions. All the clothing, blankets, weapons. It was all gone. He was left with nothing but a useless mess. *Who? Who would mess with my crew? Oh, wait they are all gone. I don't have a crew anymore.* He knelt down to sift through the mess on the ground. He saw an action figure. There were a couple of smashed and broken ones left on the ground. One was a figurine that, when twisted, would light up. He remembered that his brothers Mieko and Meiko loved this one.

The damage to his tent seemed to be beyond repair. *I can at least make the most of it.* Mato placed the ceremonial drumstick in a bare corner and grabbed all the junk he could find and put it in a giant pile. He moved anything soft to the top and everything hard to the bottom. Very few things remained that weren't nailed down, and nothing was nailed down on the reservation. He found parts of a bike, parts of action figures, parts of the bunk beds that were ripped and won't worth looting. He moved them all into his new makeshift bed. "There. Now I have something for later at least."

"Do ya?" came a high-pitched voice from behind.

"Geeko. What do you want?" Mato asked, turning to see a small figure behind him.

"Heard everyone is calling you the savior of the res. Figure you would have some protection money for me."

"What?"

"You know some money, so my boys here and I don't come by and mess some things up for you."

"Look around."

"Guess you haven't learned the first lesson of being a clone."

"Oh, what's that?"

"It can always get worse," said Geeko as he brought up a pipe to swing around. Two of his brothers rushed into the tent; they let Geeko hold their single weapon while they tried to box Mato in. *Great, now I am going to get beat up by three boys who are younger than me.* The shorter blond-haired childhood models were known for how vicious they could be. With how wildly Geeko swung the pipe, Mato knew that reputation was well deserved.

Mato ducked to the side and kicked his newly created bed at the child gangsters, slowing them down with a falling stream of junk. The sound of a pipe clanking against the ground disrupted the content hum of the electrical grid behind them. Geeko's two brothers slowed their progress. Their pale eyes pierced the dusty tent like glowing balls of hate-filled light. This gave Mato the time he needed to grab a giant ball of dirt from the ground and throw it into their eyes.

The young blond models backed away as Mato advanced. Mato could see what he needed to do. He cleared his mind of thoughts and just started to react. Grabbing the wireframe of the bunk bed behind him, he broke off a pipe of his own. Its dingy brassey color shone in the otherwise dirty environment. He replicated Geeko's earlier swings, wildly swiping from right to left, making sure to hit the ground with each swipe, causing the pipe to make a loud banging noise.

Remarkably, this swinging and banging worked, making the younger blond models run from the tent. Mato followed, yelling, and screaming to add to the effect. A crowd had formed, and Mato raised his pipe up showing them his weapon. He dared the onlookers to come at him. "Come at me!! I battled chameleon sharks, and you think you can take me! I laugh at you. Ha Ha!"

The crowd stared and muttered to themselves. They created a low rumble as everyone looked at Mato.

"You stay here. I'll be right back," Mato said.

The crowd didn't move. They seemed to be engaged in every word spoken by Mato. He went back into the tent then came out with the ceremonial drumstick. He raised both his pipe and drumstick in the air. The drumstick sparked against the pipe, sending a tickle through Mato's hand. He lowered his hands and slammed the cylinder objects against the ground creating a loud noise. He repeated this over and over until someone spoke.

"Are you a late model beater now? You saved us all and not even two days later you become a late model beater."

Mato couldn't see the clone who spoke. He appeared to be hiding from him. "I haven't yet, but I'm not afraid to. Come one, come all. Who wants to try this?" said Mato as he continued to beat the ground. The crowd soon lost interest and dispersed. He heard the crunch of a cheap plastic shoe squeak away. Mato continued to hit his sticks together and make as much noise as he could.

Eventually, clones from the neighboring tents yelled out, "Quit that shit!"

"It's over, go inside asshole."

Mato calmed down. He didn't respond to the yelling, it actually made him slightly happy. The interaction felt the most normal of everything that had happened to him lately. A smirk appeared on his face as he went inside and tried again to gather his junk, as he called it in his head, together in another pile. This time he didn't mind putting it all together. An enormous collection of crap as he thought. *Maybe I'd like being a fighter. Mato the Fighter. That doesn't sound so bad. I can't be defeated. Give me a week, and I'll be running this camp.* Mato lay against his junk with his arms crossed. *Tomorrow they will see. I'm a changed clone.*

The morning came. Mato looked in a cracked mirror, not quite sure what to do. He didn't have or hygiene products, so he just stared at himself. Studied the subtle differences that made him unique. Everyone had them, an extra dimple here, an additional mole there. They were too subtle to not confuse the Natties, but stood out like a light in the night to clones. Mato swore that he could hear another crowd outside, but he dismissed it away. *I'm just daydreaming.* Soon, he heard new noises and a challenge. This was no memory.

"Mato get out here!" shouted Geeko

"Can someone go handle that?" Mato asked of an empty room. "I forgot. I'm the only one left."

Mato lifted the cloth door to reveal Geeko had come back, this time with a makeshift ax. And he wasn't alone; he had returned with twenty late models. Not all were the same model as him, like before. This time, he saw the variety from which a person was able to order a child-like clone. Matching facings with the various different eye and hair colors. Some were different models with different builds. The chubbier clones stood up front and popped their knuckles loudly once Mato came outside. Most had pipes, and/or bats in their hands. They circled the entrance of the tent, making a unique arch of late model children clones. They all looked pre-pubescent. Everyone in the old CDF wanted a child that was still in the fun stage, teenage clones actually had the lowest sales. Clones didn't know much, but they knew about which one of them had the most worth on the previous market as well as on the current black market.

He felt glad that he had the mental presence to grab his drumstick and pipe before coming out of the tent. He reached up to start banging them against each other. *Here we go again.*

Geeko grinned as he had other plans. Geeko lifted his left leg and bent forward, charging at full speed right away. The other clones followed. They rallied behind him, presenting an almost choreographed appearance.

Mato would not be moved. He stood his ground and brought the drumstick and pipe to his sides, readied for the onslaught of children. They met him quickly. Mato blocked and dodged as many blows as he could. Geeko wildly swung like he did the day prior. Mato matched him and hit him on the head with his drumstick, leaving a sizeable red welt and watering the child's eyes. This did not do anything to change Geeko's determination. The other children moved in and hit Mato with a stick or a bat and then ran back. Mato swung, but there were few who stayed close enough to catch his blows. The drumstick started to glow. Each time he slammed the ground or hit a small late model in the back while they ran away its light grew brighter.

He tried as hard as he could to catch as many of the children when they came in for what they thought was a free hit. This fight turned into a wild bunch of flailing, quickly. Mato cried out as the repeated hits from their weapons started to make his skin sore, and his muscles ache.

The children's circle started to close in on him. They stopped running back as far with each hit they gave. The blows that they landed on Mato came more quickly. He was able to block less and less. His drumstick was glowing brightly, and it pegs came out shining in different colors. Mato's memory flashed to yesterday when he was screaming and hitting the ground in rage. Without thought, he moved his arm in an effort to repeat it. BOOM. As he smacked the ground with it, the drumstick emitted a large concussive wave that hit the children. Mato was impressed.

The children were on their backs, but not for long. If he had been surrounded by soldiers with their heavy armor and older age, Mato would have had a lot more time to recover. The youthful clones were starting to get back up and regather their weapons and now looked at him with increased interest.

A pair of chubbier clones were helping Geeko back to his feet when the child leader shout "I want that drumstick, go get it!"

Mato had faced the ferocity of chameleon sharks head-on and won. He realized he was no match for the pure evil of these children. They wanted to hurt him, and there was no stopping them, at least not head on. He had to move, get away from this situation and he had to do it fast. This was when he decided it was time to run.

Mato rushed past a late model clone, knocking him on the head with his drumstick when the clone tried to stop him. Then he stepped on the late model's stomach to get an extra boost of leverage. Rushing forward, he ran as fast as he could to get away from the group of children. Mato knocked over chairs, piles of garbage and clones selling food in his hurry to get away. He ran into a tent filled with all of the late model girls. *I should be safe there for a little while at least.*

They screamed and threw everything they had in their hands at him. They didn't know what had happened to him or who he was. They just reacted to the sudden invasion of privacy. *I better get out of here.* Running out of the tent, he saw the late model children were fast approaching.

Mato ran and ran across the reservation. The hot sun beamed down on him, and as he sweated, he kicked dust around. He felt he was in luck when the door to Eyota's condo opened. He could ditch the child clones by going in there. The late models wouldn't follow him, or if they did, he could at least double back, and they will spend all day looking for him. *I don't know what I will do tomorrow, but it doesn't matter. Today is today, and that is all I can worry about.* He rushed through the door. He tried to close it, but they were following too close to risk the delay. Entering Eyota's residence attracted the attention of the reservation's small local security. These were an unreliable volunteer force made of like-minded clones who tried to break up fights and administered any humanitarian aid they received from foreign planets. They started to grab the unruly children. Mato couldn't wait, there were too many of his pursuers, too few security guards. He ran deeper and deeper into the condo, down the stairs, past the lighted areas, and into a darkened basement. At the far end, he passed through a door into what seemed like a laboratory and underground greenroom. It was underneath the reservation, and it was vast in its scale.

Recognizing most of the fruits and vegetables, he took what looked like a peach and bit into it. Its stale underdeveloped taste was instantly familiar. This was the same fruit that they ate on a regular basis. It was unique in its muted flavor. This is where they make the food we eat. Most of the children that were after him got scared and did not follow. They didn't want to get caught raiding Eyota's place, that would not work out for them. Geeko was the only one that stayed on his trail. He followed the sounds that Mato was making and soon his target could see him behind. Geeko's face had a look of amazement.

Geeko went for the sweetest fruits he could find and started grabbing them.

"I wouldn't do that if I were you."

"Why not?" he asked.

"Last time I heard of someone stealing from Eyota, the res found their body hanging in the air with its head cut off," Mato warned.

"You're making that up. Aren't you?" Geeko questioned.

"Suit yourself," Mato replied. He shivered in the temperature-controlled room; it seemed too cold to him, even with the heat from the batteries lining the floor.

They heard strange voices and the stirring of people coming. Two distinct, heavy sets of footsteps came towards the underground green room.

"Geeko we need to hide."

The late model looked up at him and nodded in agreement. Mato grabbed Geeko's arm and dragged him behind a shelf of batteries. *These seem to be used and broken. They must be the ones waiting for replacement.*

"Shh. We can't get caught in here. The Res will string us both up as thieves." Mato stated.

"This won't change anything. I still hate you," Geeko replied.

"Save it, kid," Mato warned. His voice reduced to whisper as they saw a door open from the opposite side of the room.

Two early model clones walked through. They had on lab coats and inspected the food. They seemed more interested in the power and not how well the vegetables were doing. Their appearance was unusual for clones; they appeared much more physically fit then they should be. They looked like every clone in their model but their skin was too perfect and their clothes too clean. They just didn't seem like the right model for the reservation's scientist.

"Something doesn't feel right Geeko." Geeko again looked up and nodded. "I know it in the pit of my stomach something is wrong." The two early models started talking.

"I don't see any defense grids," the first one said.

"We have our mission, and I'll be dammed if we don't fulfill it. You know our orders came straight from the stop."

"That's not good. I can't find anything."

"This disguise is killing me can we take it off. I think it will help me look around, Castor."

"Absolutely not. Doing so will make you subject to treason charges. We got to put up with it until the job is done," replied the clone named Castor.

Geeko looked up and this time had an evil grin. Mato immediately grabbed him. "I don't know what you are thinking but don't," Mato whispered harshly.

"Let go they are here to do a caper. I want in on this."

"No, you don't," replied Mato.

"If I can get in with the early models I'll be set. You wouldn't know you are a good clone now," he replied.

Mato let go but a little too quickly. Geeko slammed into the batteries causing them to shift and make several shuffling sounds followed by the slam of Geeko falling.

"Who's there?" One of the early models asked.

"Come out if you know what is good for ya."

Both of the early models reached for their side. But there was nothing there at least nothing Mato could see. Geeko got up and emerged from behind the batteries.

"It's me Geeko. I know you have heard of me. I know you are here for a caper and I want in."

Both of the early models laughed, their hands never leaving their sides. They belted out a couple of loud chuckles then returned to normal.

"Get out of here kid. This doesn't concern you," the shorter of the clones said.

Geeko stomped in his feet in frustration. "I mean it. I can help with whatever you are doing here. I know things. Things I shouldn't know," Geeko stated.

The two clones raised their eyebrows. "Is anyone with you?"

You better not rat me out. He balled his fist, getting ready to fight it out if he had to.

"Nope, just me," Geeko said raising his upper lip in nervous smugness.

"I'm Castor, and this is Nez. Nice to meet you, little one. We are looking for a glowing green ball that is sometimes covered in what looks like bronze and circuitry. What do you know of it?"

Nez elbowed Castor "The kid won't know what bronze is."

"It kind of looks like a dirty gold," Castor reiterated.

Geeko moved a finger to his chin and tapped his feet, obviously thinking about it. "I've heard rumors of secret rooms in old man Eyota's apartment. Maybe there is more down here than stale food? I'm small and scrappy; I can find this gold thing you are looking for no problem. I'm not slow like you old people," said Geeko

"Watch it with the 'old people' kid," said Castor

"Sorry," replied Geeko.

The pair of late models looked at each and seemed to speak with their eyes. They relaxed and finally let their arms fall from the awkward positions above their waists. Finally relaxed, the shorter clone spoke up. "All right kid. Let's see what you can do."

"You talk funny, are you from a different reservation?" said Geeko

"Focus kid. Mind your business," said the taller clone, breaking his recent bout of silence.

"Now just wait. I might be an early model, but I don't do anything for free. What's in it for me?"

"We won't..." Castor let out a small gasp as he was nudged in the side from the taller clone. "We will split the profit with you."

"We will? "the taller clone asked. Castor turned back and gave him a quick wink. "Of course, we will. You can trust us kid."

Mato slowly tried to back out of the hiding spot and crawl for the other side of the room where there was another door. He didn't know if it was locked, but Mato wanted to get out of this situation. His fighter instincts were telling him that this wasn't one that he could win with his ceremonial drumstick.

Geeko turned to move closer to the late model clones marching by, lifting his legs entirely to his waist in a comedically exaggerated manner. The late model clones were not amused; they frowned quickly but raised their lips back up to fake smiles at the young child looking clone. This changed back as soon as a second rumbling came from the battery rack.

"Whoa, are you running a game on us kid?" The taller clone asked.

Geeko didn't respond, he turned and ran towards Mato. Mato, knowing that the time to be sneaky had passed, got up and ran for the inner door. The two clones rushed together in a sprint, laser blasts searing the air. Missed shots made flower pots explode, creating the sharp sound of broken ceramics in the room. The noise echoed, and small fires were started.

The late model clones tried to shoot the pair. They stood in relaxed stances firing shot after shot. They didn't take the time to aim. They rushed their shots, overconfident that their training and skill would guide them.

"Where did they get the blasters from?" Mato asked Geeko, breathlessly. Geeko looked up and shook his head. Mato smacked the keypad frantically as planters kept exploding around them. Mato attempted to calm himself, and when he did, he saw the button that was labeled "OPEN." It was in an obvious place. He slammed his fist on it, almost breaking the entire panel. Clearing the door, Mato rushed into a stairway that led upward. It spiraled and was made out of slick, glossy material. He climbed upward, not bothering to look back in fear of catching a stray laser bolt to the face. Mato could hear some kind of strange high pitch sound, but he could barely make it out. In what felt like an hour, but was only minutes, he had made it all the way up what was several flights of stairs. He pushed open another door, not panicking at the keypad like before, and found himself outside. He looked back in an attempt to wait for Geeko, but he didn't see him. *That is odd.* Mato's thought was interrupted by a laser blast. The clones were shooting straight up at him from the bottom of the stairs. Mato had to go.

Mato tried to run in the direction of his home tent, but he was grabbed by the elder. "Come with me. It's started."

"What? I have to go, people are after me," said Mato.

"You young people so dramatic. No one is after you boy," the elder said.

"No there really is. A couple of late models, they had blasters, and I lost Geeko."

"If you can handle all those sharks like they said you did you can handle a couple of late models. Wait, late models? I thought you were having troubles with early models? Oh, it doesn't matter you need to get to the surface level. The rain festival is about to start. Do you have the special drumstick that I gave you?"

Mato couldn't believe it, but it was in his hand. He hadn't let go, even after running through the underground greenroom and being shot at. It glowed brightly. It had been fully charged. It must have gotten energized while he was running away.

"Oh, great you charged it. Keep it that way," said the elder. The elder and his escort of late model clones took Mato and escorted him to the tent of the Elder Clones.

The Elder Clone's tent wasn't much nicer than all the normal tents, it was just bigger. It was also arranged quite differently. It was circular, and the elder women sat in a small circle while the elder men sat in a larger circle around them. Bunk beds lined the walls, and their top corners supported the tent. Once Mato entered, everyone turned and looked over the young man before returning to their business. There was a haze of white smoke that filled the air. Mato recognized the smell; it was a bramble weed, a mild natural depressant that was native to the planet. Mato watched as the elders smoked it from a small ceramic pipe which they passed around. It was so quiet that he could hear the clicking sound of the lighter that lit the plant while the elders burned it.

The elderly women waved to Mato, motioning for him to sit in the center of the circle. Mato compiled and sat down. All eyes were on him, and he did not know what to do.

He had never been in the Elder's tent. He hadn't had a need to. *This is a strange new experience.*

"Join and smoke the bramble plant with us. It will calm you down. We can't have you starting anymore fights right now," the lead elder commanded.

"Start fights? That's unfair; everyone was coming after me. I'm not starting these fights. I'm finishing them," Mato protested.

"This is why we need you to smoke," the elder replied.

The pipe moved from the back circle, passed from person to person until it reached Mato in the center. A small electric lighter was given with it as well. Mato took the two items and brought the pipe to his lips. He lit it in a similar fashion to what he saw the elders do. He choked and coughed loudly. The elder women who were closest to him laughed. Their neutral-colored, long dresses contrasted against the vast tapestry rug that had been laid on the floor. It had a geometric design and was apparently stolen from one of the old casinos.

"Good, breath it in slowly child," said the lead elder. Mato did as he was told. Soon, time started to slow down in his head. His thoughts took longer, and everyone seemed to be speaking closer.

"Do you have any food?" he asked.

A tray was passed, again from the outer circle, until it reached him.

"I know the fame of saving the reservation is a sudden and great thing. We ask that you use it for good and don't let it go to your head. We need you to calm down and stop with this fighting. We don't have much time before the rain starts, and the reservation must work as one during the collection process," the lead elder stated.

"It's not me," Mato replied.

"Regardless, that is not how clones treat other people," the elder replied.

"Respect your clone brothers and sisters. No one has it rougher than us in this galaxy," said one of the elder ladies.

"I do. I appreciate the wisdom of everyone in this room, but I was the only one with the sense to save Eyota and the rest of our asses..."

Mato was interrupted by a smack in the back of the head. He turned to see an elder woman giving him a wicked sneer.

He turned back around and continued on. "Saved all our butts. Maybe I should be the elder."

"Listen, child. Stay out of trouble. The gratitude for saving Eyota will only go so far. You are already finding out how hard life can be when you have no one on your side," said one of the old men, pointing a stern finger at him.

"I think I understand," Mato replied. *I understand that I'm sitting in a room full of fools.*

"Good. Now let's go to Eyota's. He is waiting for you," the old man continued.

The blood drained from Mato's face. He was surprised that Eyota could be back at his house and that he was going back there. Mato got up and headed for the tent's entrance. He was surprised at how late it had gotten. It was already night time again.

The Elder turned Mato around and pointed him in the direction of Eyota's front door. There were lots of late models, and they all were hunched over as they danced in celebration of the rain ceremony.

Mato was pushed past the dancers and back into Eyota's apartment. This time he walked in slowly. He had time to look at all in the in-set lighting. The glass and marble stone interior looked vibrant and gave a luxurious look to the meeting space. Mato was rushed passed the central greeting area and into a conference room. There sat a fat man with olive colored skin and long hair. He was eating a large meal, barely stopping to acknowledge Mato at all. Eyota stood in the middle of the room next to the long wooden conference table looking at a datapad.

"Glad you can join me in my house again. Did you and your little friend have fun?" said Eyota. Mato was shocked that Eyota could know about this and be so casual so nonchalant about his earlier skirmish in his home.

"Yeeea. Sorry about the mess. Do I owe you somehow?" said Mato

"Don't worry about it. Just make sure it doesn't happen again. You are only to come when invited. We conduct sensitive meetings in here so I can't have you just running in whenever you want," chided Eyota.

"I won't do it again," Mato replied.

"Do you know who this man is?" Eyota asked. Mato shook his head.

"I'm The Lord Hate my boy," he said as he smacked his lips. "Come, why don't you talk to me for a second."

"I would rather not," said Mato

"You don't want to know how to be famous? How to make more money than you can possibly imagine? You see this place? You can have one exactly like it if you do well."

He sat back in his chair straightening his back. Although he was looking up from his seated position, it felt to Mato as though the lord was staring down on him from high above. His long, black hair was pulled up in a ponytail, and his face was done up in what appeared to be very obvious and poorly done makeup.

"The clones you take away never come back and I rather not be another one of them," said Mato.

"You think anyone wants to come back to this shithole after the riches I show them?" asked Lord Hate. Mato didn't reply, but he knew that Lord Hate had a point.

"I let you offer your service to the boy, and he refused. We'll discuss other business later. I still have some local issues to straighten out with the child," said Eyota.

He grabbed Mato by the shoulder and lead him away into another conference room that was about two doors down from the one they were just in.

"That guy is a creep," said Mato once he was confident they were speaking in quiet. He wasn't sure, but the burden of holding in the comment just overtook him. "If he were a clone, I would just punch him in the face."

"I'm sure you would," said Eyota as he sat down behind his desk. Mato could see numerous awards that Eyota had earned while working with the clones. His activities at the reservation gained him a lot of recognition in humanitarian communities.

"I fear that instead of saving me you just pushed out my death a little," stated Eyota.

"What does that mean? Do you need me to go fight Lord Hate for you? I'll take one for the reservation, I don't care if I die," replied Mato.

"No, it's nothing that blunt. I don't need a hammer for this problem. Maybe a velvet glove with a hammer underneath," said Eyota

"I can't understand you. Why are you speaking in riddles?" said Mato.

"I'll just say it. I think Lord Hate has spied on the reservation. He landed with more crew than I can account for, and two of them are missing. He is rather evasive about it, and I think you might be good for the job of finding out what he is up to. Do you know that he is an Acolyte?"

"An Acolyte, here? Why haven't we killed him? We can't have Acolytes running around the Res!!"

Mato thought back to the stories of how The Acolytes swore to cleanse the galaxy of clones. They were the destroyers of The Clone Defense Force, the only government which stood for their representation. The only reason they needed a reservation was because of them. Clones required someplace to call their own after The Acolytes proceeded to conquer, plunder, or destabilize any planet that was previously under CDF control.

"We can't have Acolytes running around the reservation, that is exactly right. What Lord Hate does here isn't, well, let's just say there are things that need to happen, things that some people will have trouble with. Business has been going smoothly, but a man like that is not to be trusted blindly," said Eyota

"I'll get to the bottom of it," said Mato

"No, you won't. You will just, and I say just, report anything strange you see to the elders. Can you do that?" asked Eyota.

Mato nodded.

"Things are changing around here quickly. Not only is Lord Hate here, but the rain is starting, and he warns of another group of visitors. Let's just hope we are intact when they all leave." Screens behind Eyota started turning red with a small beeping alarm, and a picture formed of small red symbols approaching what appeared to a depiction of the planet on the monitor behind him.

"What's that?" Mato asked.

"Speak of the devil. The rain, it's starting. Take your drumstick and meet the honor guard on the cliffs. Do you know the spot?" said Eyota.

"Yes, every clone does," said Mato.

"Off you go then."

Mato was dressed in full honor guard gear. Shorts, a half shirt, fluffy boots, and now he held two drumsticks. He stood among the rest of the guards as they waited for the rain to actually start. They were split up into three groups of six people. Each group stood to wait at different points along the circular cliffs that surrounded the large pit that made up the reservation. The land above the reservation was flat, so they could see the other groups, but they were just tiny figures in the distance. Mato couldn't make out much except for the occasional wave. Whenever that happened, the other guards would look at him and wait for him to wave back. *The price of fame.* He looked over and saw someone new coming out of the access point.

The access point was about 500 feet away. It looked like it was a hole in the ground. In reality, it was an extended set of ascending stairs and ladders that led to the surface. Mato didn't care much for the surface. The abandoned casinos and the flats that ran into jungles that ran into sand then water. Mato believed he had all he needed back at the reservation; life outside of it was dangerous and lonely. Besides who would he fight if there was no one around?

A small white hand appeared climbing up from the access point.

Mato looked over at the honor guard. "Is anyone else coming? I thought there were only our three groups."

"No one else is supposed to be here, no," said the honor guard member.

"Looks like someone doesn't care about the rules," Mato replied.

They all shared a laugh at the notion that the rules should apply so strictly. Then more than a hand appeared over the access point's edge. It was a small face.

"Geeko!" Mato blurted out.

"You are still fighting that kid?" said the honor guard Mato was speaking to before.

"He followed you all the way here?" said another.

"Late models don't give up."

This starting another round of laughter from the group. Geeko got his footing then two more hands appeared behind him.

"If Geeko wants a fight. I'll give it to him," Mato stated.

"Don't take too long we need you for the rain," said the captain of the honor guard. He was slightly taller and more muscular than the rest. He stood out in the uniformed group.

Geeko pointed in their direction. Mato could not tell if he was just pointing, pointing at him individually, or pointing at the group. Mato saw the two other people that followed and recognized them as the older clones from before. He thought about the situation for a moment. These clones were quite strange. There must be something more to them. They climbed over the edge of the access point and then reached for their sides. Still, Mato could not see what they were reaching for, it just looked they were grabbing for air until suddenly two blasters appeared, and the clones started shooting. A blaster bolt came right at him. Mato closed his eyes and waited for the pain, for the cold silence of the end of his life. This didn't happen; he just heard a very faint swooping sound. *What was that? I've never heard anything like it.* Mato opened his eyes to see the fact that the captain had saved him. He had placed his drumstick in front of Mato's face, absorbing the blast. The two clones from before kept firing, squeezing the triggers until their guns overheated and the hot metal glowed. The Honor guard surrounded Mato absorbing the explosion with their drumsticks, charging them until they also glowed. This was quite odd looking. Mato was sure they looked like some clone dance crew and not a decorated honor guard. Both sides of the confrontation stood with glowing weapons. They both appeared to be waiting for them to cool down naturally. Then the rain started.

What looked to be new stars appeared in the night's sky above them. Acolyte ships hovering above the planet. They fired their batteries, shooting directly down at the reservation. Explosions occurred all across the island. The flats were hit, and explosions started happening all around them. Mato's ears rang from the noise. Dust was kicked up, and fireballs seemed to appear in all directions. Mato could see the green lasers fall from the sky and wreak their havoc on the jungle that circled the flats. The bombardment wasn't guided, so it started wildfires sometimes even demolished one of the casinos.

The Honor guard moved into action. They turned their back on the strange clones and slammed their drumsticks on the ground to propel themselves over the cliffs. Only Mato, the strange clones from earlier, Geeko, and the captain of the honor guard remained.

"Let this go. The reservation needs you now. The rain has started!"

Mato was still facing the strange clones. He ignored Geeko. The late model was not really a concern at this moment to him.

"I want to fight. I can take them. Now that I know what the drumsticks can do. They don't stand a chance," Mato explained.

"They'll explode if you overload them. We don't have time for this. The lives of the entire reservation are on the line."

"But Eyota told me to watch out for those two. I need to fight them. It's my mission."

"Not right now, it's not." The captain grew frustrated with arguing. He grabbed Matos hand with his own and pulled him into a tight hug. Taking the combined four drumsticks, he slammed all four against the ground, and then did a backflip over the cliffs, taking Mato with him.

Geeko and the strange clones watched in awe at the skill and sheer athleticism such a move would take. The blasters of the strange clones finally cooled down enough for additional shots, but they couldn't think to shoot by the time the last two honor guard was over the cliffs and gone.

Chapter 3

Such a passionate and forceful kiss. Leanne tried to resist, but that was met with more chasing. She felt her pursers enjoyed it more when she resisted. Leanne wondered if there was a point in continuing her resistance. It was strange how her pursuer could be so strong. Leanne was slighter bigger than her pursuer she thought about trying to use her weight and overpowering her. That almost worked once, but that just led to a beating, something she did not want to repeat. She passively stood there as Dark Cleo kissed her passionately. Too passionately.

There was nothing wrong with Dark Cleo. She was still a beautiful woman, but that was the problem. She wasn't what Leanne wanted. She was too loud too strict. Nothing like the princes Leanne dreamed of. Leanne was trained on how to please a man. Dark Cleo presented something that she didn't understand. Duty called to her and Leanne knew her place. She was to be the excellent wife of Dark Cleo. This had already brought power and gravitas to her family. She wasn't doing this for love or personal pleasure, so she needed to get those concepts out of her head and kiss back. Regardless, she didn't feel the urge or match Dark Cleo's mood tonight. All the signs were there. A long and slow song played in the background. The bed was made with rose petals from Planet Terry in all the colors that Leanne hated but told Cleo were fine. Leanne knew how to cool down most of the males she ran into. It was rather easy, just holovid a sport, ply them with alcohol and next thing you know they were fast asleep. Dark Cleo was different. She mostly behaved like the ladies she knew, but harder and sometimes she acted like the males. Whenever they would talk about those rose petals, her time on Planet Terry and why she liked them so much Dark Cleo would shut down. *That is if I could bring up Planet Terry again. No, that would be too obvious. I wish I could just give her a bunch of alcohol, but Dark Cleo didn't drink. She preferred to keep her mind clear for battle strategy, she said.*

Dark Cleo reached for a drawer next to the bed. It glowed in a vivid maroon color matching the rose petals on the bed. Leanne thought to back away, but there wasn't much room in their quarters of the underground facility where they dwelled. The room was cold and grey "like our marriage," she thought. The only color was the bed the nightstands that were attached to, and the rose petals which Dark Cleo flung all over the place.

"Not tonight honey," Leanne spoke up.

"You say that every night," Dark Cleo replied.

Leanne's eyes turned towards their wedding picture. A large moving photo hovered above their bed. It reminded her of their wedding day even when she was reluctant, but she didn't know how naive she had been marrying Dark Cleo.

Now was the time for Leanne to think of something. Dark Cleo continued to reach in their drawer, and Leanne knew precisely what she was getting. A synthetic device that is capable of impregnation. It converted the cells of the wearer to an artificial sperm. Dark Cleo was always rougher than average when she wore it. Leanne suspected some type of role play was going on in Cleo's head. Cleo was an athletic warrior, and she didn't tire out easily, so Leanne felt the need to prevent the night of torture that was coming into existence. It was actually something Leanne remembered laughing about with the other princesses she knew when they went on the galactic web. It and other extreme devices seemed so vulgar and low class.

"You know you can always go marry God-Wrath. I hear he needs to make it an even dozen."

"That's not funny."

"It is what it is."

Leanne tried to keep a cool head. She went from not in the mood to actively angry. She hated how she did her best thinking under these circumstances.

"Isn't the fight tonight? Are you going to let your pets just run wild without their leash?" Dark Cleo got up and slammed the drawer of the dresser and stared down Leanne.

"You have a duty," she said, then turned and stormed out of the room.

Chapter 4

.... A short while later while Dark Cleo strolled through the facility...

Leanne had a point, even if Dark Cleo didn't want to admit it. The clones her family rescued from Novus had grown up, and now they were fighting the central hexagon. They had strange abilities, and when left alone they got into trouble quickly. Dark Cleo watched the fish as she power walked through the facility. Giant glass windows showed the lake and all of its beautiful creatures. It was a beautiful sight to see school of long and short fish, even smaller octopus that would float across. The view allowed a person to look across at the other side of the facility. Below lay the production plant and in the middle were the spaceships. They were being built like submarines in a beehive. Dark Cleo rushed towards one of the three bridges that allowed a person to go directly across the facility instead of going a long way around. They were glass bridges that had a large hexagon observation room. It allowed technicians to watch the progress of the ship production.

The facility had its beauty, but Dark Cleo would have preferred to build her fleet out in the open. The clandestine nature of the facility made it much slower than if she just made them in a regular shipyard, but God-Wrath couldn't know about this. If the fleet didn't enrage him back into open war, the fact that there were clones, especially ones that contained some of his DNA, would make him supernova. Even Dark Cleo in her quest for revenge didn't want to bring that down on herself, at least not yet. Not until she abandoned this facility with her fleet, ready to strike. Even then she might the keep the clones secret. She had seen firsthand how radical a cause God-Wrath considered their elimination.

Galactic Mandate: The Scream

Reaching the second bridge, she entered the long hallway, passing guards standing watch over the night's R&R activity. The clones Variant and Fractal were going to fight. This brought most of the base who wanted to watch away from the first and third bridge, as the second was where the fight was being held. The base considered this to be the main event. People exchanged cash in bets, and special speakers and monitors were brought in so everyone in the hexagons and even those who couldn't leave their critical stations could watch. Dark Cleo also heard some had sold tickets for the spots on the hexagons to watch the fight live. A practice she thought she should crack down on, but it never made that top of her list of things to do. The men need some distraction. Dark Cleo looked down to see the lights of spaceships that were newly constructed, each in their hexagon pods. She looked to her right and saw the wall of pods and the glass of the facility that lined the top. The activities of the workers stood out because of the brightness of the rooms and the darkness of the water. It highlighted what they were doing here.

As Dark Cleo reached the hexagon, guards moved out of her way and closed rank behind her. Cleo leaned into the wall and ran fingers through her hair and touched the shaved left side of her head. It was almost time for Variant and Fractal to begin.

Chapter 5

Mato was in mid backflip when the leader of the honor guard pulled away. The rest of the guard were already pounding at giant drums that lined the top of the cliff. Mato fell into what was a contest and a dance. The honor guard fell onto the drums and using their drumsticks they were able to bounce from one drum to another flying in the air. The purpose of this drumming was to activate the sonic grid.

The spaceship fired their batteries from high above shooting blast after blast of green lasers. The ones that would have made a direct hit on the reservation, causing devastation, and killing all the clones, were suspending in the air due to the efforts of the honor guard, using the drums and their drumsticks. The drummers had to pay attention and adjust which drums they went to depending on what was happening with the green lasers. There was a delicate balance. Drumming too hard on the larger and more powerful drums would reverse the blast, and it would bounce off the reservation. The blast wouldn't go too far just jump up and over, causing more destruction in the surrounding area. Drumming just enough would cause the blast to suspend, neither hitting the reservation nor causing destruction around it.

Mato was a natural. He hit the drums and paid attention to the laser blast so that the reservation could harvest its energy. That was the goal of the rain ceremony. The more energy they harvested, the more they could repair the surrounding area. With each hit of the drums, it amplified the energy released, moving like a wave until it would hit the green blast and wrap around it like a velvet glove.

Mato was conflicted. On the one side, he was happy he went to protect his reservation once more and engage in this rather trying but undoubtedly fun physical activity. On the other, he yearned to fight the spies that he was sure had become Geeko's friends. This conflict filled his head as he and the rest of the honor guard bounced from drum to drum, first the bigger, then the smaller ones to refine the harvest of energy. Once the power would start to glow and start to become unstable from the transformation, a group of clones on the ground would finish the job.

They had what looked like a giant bagpipe. The collection bag dragged on the ground, and it took the strength of twenty people to move it. It took another six-man crew to operate. There were those who moved that bag as it was wheeled on the ground and those who blew into a long tube. It made a high pitch noise and sucked the energy from the green laser blast like a vacuum. Mato didn't have time to watch or look at the clones collecting the energy. He knew what they did with it. They would reverse the electrical grid and put it in the large batteries that were housed in the casinos.

Mato thought about the early models, and what they had told him how the rain made them feel. It was something that caused him great sadness whenever he thought about it. The energy from the physical activity met his thoughts and fought for supremacy. Mato could not help but remember what the late models and his fallen brothers had said. He used to tell stories about the ceremonies with his roommates, and they would speculate about why it was happening and if it was better if it stopped it or kept going.

"If the rain never comes, we would have no power," said Mieko.

"The elders hate the devastation and the cleanup. Every year we have to rebuild and rehab the land. It's just not worth it."

"Eyota should find a way to move us somewhere else."

"I just wish it would stop."

"God-Wrath already won the war against us. What else does he want?"

"We should organize a new great clone defense force. We will rise again, just you wait. Eyota told me that he had the connections. We could do it."

"I think that is why God-Wrath keeps sending the ships."

"We would be better off if it never happened. Then we could build a power plant and just live our lives in peace."

"What's peace?" Mato asked the ghosts in his head. He never questioned it in person just a modification of his memory. Or was it an error?

Eyota looked up at the rain ceremony from the protection of his condo. He showed a proud grin. He was pleased that the clones were doing exactly what he had taught them. They took his knowledge, and they ran with it. They had created something more than he could ever imagine. *I'll have to bring that Mato in and see if he has found anything yet. Those spies can't be up to any good.* Eyota thought. With the clones being busy protecting their homes he waited alone. Only Lord Hate remained, with his entourage in a separate guest quarter. Eyota went back to his office to admire his decorations and accolades that he had received helping out the clones, imparting them with his culture. When they first arrived here, they had nothing. The CDF dumped them and ran before they themselves were hunted down into nonexistence. Another alarm, this one beeped slightly differently than the others. It was a proximity alarm for the ground. A ship was approaching, a small well-armed shuttle. Eyota typed in some commands on his console. This opened up a camera to get a closer look at the shuttle. It said Death's Witness on the side.

"They are here. And it's a horrible time. I'll have to keep them separate from Lord Hate, or we are done for!" He exclaimed to himself.

Chapter 6

Jay departed the shuttle. He looked over the Reservation while getting details from his personal mission assistant. He was the oldest of the current team. Stopping for a moment, he thought about what had happened. Death's Witness had grown over the years. It had evolved and changed. No longer did they answer to Dark Reign. Not that anyone really answered to Dark Reign anymore. They had many masters; whoever had enough coin and wasn't a zealot was the rule. Being a mercenary wasn't as fulfilling, some said, but it had its days. Some of their skills had atrophied, but they were still the best around. *Now is no time to reminisce.* Jay looked around and brought out his team which was one of many in the new organization.

The new job didn't demand much. Rough up a few clones, find the circuit. Working for a scientist was usually easy. They didn't have the demands of a warlord, or a government trying to do something below the brow. Once nice thing about being a merc working for a scientist was that they now had state of the art equipment. He just wished the younger recruits would have had the training to use it. They treated anyone new and fresh like it was almost disposable. It was a harsh reality that he didn't like thinking about. *But hey this is the way it is.* If they didn't prove their worth, he didn't have the time to trust them or treat them with the respect they deserved. *A newbie in this field can get you killed. I have seen it before, and it won't happen again. At least not on my watch.*

"Claire. Do you have anything you wanted to say about the mission," Jay asked.

She looked out at the reservation and replied. "Yes. Acolytes have a clandestine presence here. They are trying to undermine the defense grid. If that happens, our jobs will become much harder almost impossible. "

"I don't think the scientist can afford the hazard rate if that happens, so let's keep it cheap for her all right. She is kind of cute, and I'm hoping for a date, so I want everyone to get in and out fast."

"Oh, I bet you do."

Everyone shared a good-natured laugh. The sound did not travel far in the ruined landscape.

"Don't worry boss we will find the circuit and get you home in time to ask the scientist to dinner. "

"I'd be careful. You don't want her making you into her lab rat, do you?" one of the recruits asked

Jay's eye grew big. He was genuinely astounded. Back in the military days, no one would have talked to his commander like that, even with the looser rules of Death's Witness. These recruits, they were something different than he was used to. *Let's just hope they last long enough for it to matter.*

Mato watched Geeko like a hawk from afar. Geeko was talking with the collectors, so some must have been his friends. They had not finished returning the large collection bag unit to its secret storage facility. Mato surmised that Geeko must be getting close with the collectors so they would tell him where it was. *Whatever the spies are looking for must be there.*

Geeko appeared to chat more with the collection crew. He smiled and really seemed to charm them. Before long, Geeko was pushing the tail end of the bag and helping the team push it through the reservation. Mato blended in with the crowd. He grabbed a dark tan cloak with a hood and draped it over himself to provide some cover. He needed something to hide his face and any distinguishable features from Geeko. He didn't want Geeko or the collection crew to get suspicious, that would most likely ruin his plans to catch the spies. *Geeko must be working with them now. If I can follow him, he will lead me right to them.*

The collectors lead Geeko to a strange tent that didn't look big enough to hold the five clones and the collection bag at the same time. It sat on a small hill that Mato never really noticed before. There appeared to be secrets about the reservations that even Mato didn't know. The clones opened the tent drape, revealing a glimpse of what looked like a secret passage, but Mato couldn't tell. He would have to get closer before he could confirm it. Geeko helped push the collection bag through, and he seemed to just be another member of the crew at this point. As they proceeded inside, they disappeared from Mato's point of view.

Mato waited for a couple of minutes. He didn't want to wait too long and lose the trail or wait too little and have the collection crew notice him. When the time came, he went forward and followed them into the mysterious tent. Nothing was there, just some junk and an obvious secret passage underground with large rock colored doors. They were large but very light and easy to move. This made sense because the collection crews couldn't run the collection bags and handle a heavy door at the same time. They would need more clones for that, and it was a need to know job only.

When Mato entered the passage, he saw the collection crew turn a corner down another hallway. *What a stroke of good luck. If I had been a minute earlier, they would have seen me.* Mato rushed to catch up and peer his head around the corner so he could see where they were headed.

The collectors headed down the hallway until they reached a clearing room with the other collection bags. They were already put away, and Mato could see the space where the last packet was missing. Various wires hung from the wall. The trained collection crew grabbed cables and wires from all directions. The crew moved like a well-maintained machine. Geeko slipped away while looking to the ceiling. He had found what looked to be the primary electrical vein. It was hooked up to all the bags and clicked and pulsated as it drained them. The collection crew didn't notice Geeko moving towards the center of the facility and slipping away from them. They were so busy doing what they were trained to do that they didn't notice anything else. *Now is my chance.* He swiftly moved away and around the collection crew to pursue Geeko. Mato made sure his moves were swift and silent. He couldn't afford to be slowed down by the busy workers.

Hot on Geeko's trail, Mato moved down stone hallways littered in electronics and wires, chasing the late model clone who had run out of sight. Without anything else to go on, Mato looked up and followed the same electrical vein that he saw Geeko following. This worked like a guiding light through a confusing maze of hallways and rooms. Mato passed what looked like other greenrooms, and it finally clicked. *The collection process is how we survive. I better make sure it doesn't get brought down by a little kid.* Following the vein, he was led into what felt like a refrigerator.

It was a small cold room that was covered in hastily painted white paint. There were a couple of computer panels that obviously controlled what was in the middle of the room. A circuit, floating atop a large spire that came up from the ground. Another spire came from the ceiling to match it. Energy flowed from the top and changed colors, then it entered the bottom spire. It appeared as a green light that transformed into a blue one.

Geeko was standing by a red lever that said emergency ejection above it. He put on a giant rubber glove that was apparently too big for him and reached towards it.

"No don't."

Geeko turned towards the sudden interruption. "What are you doing here?" He asked with a confused look.

Mato ran towards him, cutting the distance in half in just a second. Geeko eyes grew big turning his shocked response into a fight or flight. This time it wasn't going to be a fight, and Geeko knew it. He stopped fussing with his glove, grabbed the lever, and everything went   black.

Chapter 7

Jay was in a meeting with a very nervous Eyota.

"You know we have to at least seem neutral here. We really don't want to be on God-Wrath's radar more than we already are," said Eyota.

"Neutral. He wants to wipe you out. Besides we don't have a side. We are independent contractors," said Jay.

"I don't know if The Acolytes will see it that way," said Eyota.

"I tell you what. You scratch my back, and I'll scratch yours. I know you don't want any trouble. My boys outside, they can start some at any time."

Eyota swallowed the spit in his mouth loudly. He was sweating and dabbing his forehead to relieve some of the stress. "You can have full reign of the camp, anything you need just let us know," said Eyota.

"Hey I heard that," said Claire in Jay's communicator. Jay had to ignore it for the moment.

"That is more like it," said Jay. The power went out. "Looks like you need our help more than you thought."

"If you would excuse me. I have urgent internal matters to attend to," said Eyota in the dark. Emergency lights clicked on ending the darkness.

"Hunting Acolytes, right? You are in luck. That is what my team is especially good at," said Jay.

"I thought you didn't pick sides anymore," said Eyota.

"We don't, but I still have my personal favorites," Jay said with a smile and a wink. "Now who do you have tracking those clone haters? Who should my team coordinate with?"

"I have a young man named Mato tracking them down. He's the hero of the reservation. He even saved my life," said Eyota.

Jay tried his best to hold back laughter. Although he was a success, it took a considerable amount of effort not to disrespect the magistrate of the reservation who being as cooperative he could be.

Eyota gritting his teeth grabbed his walkie and talked into it.

"Where is Mato? … Find him and bring him to me…. Yes again."

Chapter 8

Mato tried to fight Geeko but he was slippery, and it was hard to see in the underground facility with the lights off. When the emergency lights came back on, Mato noticed Geeko had the circuit in his hand. He gave a childish salute and ran away. Mato gave chase, but it was no use. Without something to guide him through the maze, it was too easy to get lost, which he did. Mato couldn't see the ceiling, and he could only barely see what was around him. He could tell that the facility didn't have much power because some of the lights faded and it kept getting dimmer as he ran around.

No longer looking for Geeko, just trying to find his way back, Mato decided to only make right turns. He heard somewhere that would lead you out of any maze. He wondered if what he heard on random holovision shows was correct. He knew he couldn't trust them too much because almost nothing they said about clones was ever real. Eventually, Mato came to a large metal door. He hadn't seen many entries like it, so he decided to give it a chance. This was the right decision as it led to the outside, where local security seemed to be waiting for him.

"We got him," they called in.

The blackout was worse than Mato had thought. It wasn't just the underground facility all the power all over was cut. Mato could see clones trying to replug-in and fiddle with wires to get the power to work on their various devices.

Mato saw a glimpse of Geeko looking back at him, smiling due to Mato's arrest.

"Grab that late model!" He screamed to no avail.

"Oh, isn't that your little buddy? We heard all about your trouble with him," the guards laughed.

"Should we take the little one?" asked the guard on the left.

"Yes!!! Grab him. He's a spy!" This caused the guards to laugh again. They no longer entertained the idea and dragged Mato away.

Mato was brought before Eyota and another tall, well-built man. He had bulging muscles, dark brown skin that contrasted against the clone's lighter tones. He also had short buzzed cut hair and a wicked grin. His black military gear had a name tag that said "Jay."

"I hear you can tell me where The Acolytes are, is that true?" Jay leaned down and towered over the boy.

"Maybe if you hadn't sent these guards to get me," Mato muttered back.

"Don't try me, boy. Tell me everything you know now."

Mato looked up defiant and proud. "I was following a late model Geeko…"

"This is the leader of a Death's Witness squad," Eyota broke in. "He is here on a dangerous mission and doesn't want to hear about your schoolyard troubles. Do you have any news for us or not?"

"That is what I'm trying to tell you. Geeko he is working with the spies. I know it. They look like clones, but they have these invisible guns."

"Clones? We are asking about Acolyte spies. Take him away. I'm disappointed in you. I thought you could handle something more than childish games after what you did when we were on the ocean, but I see now that you are just not ready." Eyota said

"Wait delay that command," Jay said

"Excuse me? In just what is your mission here Jay? Why do you think you can you override me in my domain?"

"Shut it before I break your face," answered Jay. Jay reached for his ear and his communicator. "Claire scan the area. I just got word The Acolytes are using a local holo-cloak." Jay said over the Death's Witness communication channel.

"I found two signals…. Wait this isn't good. Looks like they are going for a ship that is parked just outside the reservation on the other side. We can't get there in time. You are on your own Jay." Claire responded.

Jay relayed the information to the group around him.

"Shit, Geeko got a circuit from an underground lab. He must be giving it to the spies, that must have been what they were after," said Mato.

Jay looked the administrator. "There is not much we can do about it unless we get some transportation. This is your domain. Get us something to outrun your spies, or it's over for you Eyota."

"We have some wheeled motorbikes. I give them to the clones to play on since we don't have any real hover bikes here. No one knows the res like you Mato. Can you show Jay what he needs?" said Eyota.

The guards released Mato. "Gladly. Follow me, chump," said Mato as he raced away.

A grin was on Jay's face as he watched the young man rush away from him. He gave chase, following the clone.

Mato rushed down alleys, through and around tents, quickly maneuvering around clones that were in his way. Jay, by contrast, bulldozed over anything that was foolish enough not to move out of his way. Jay held back; he didn't have any ill will towards the clones, he just wanted them out of his way so he would toss anyone who didn't understand what was going on to the side. He did this quickly in an abrasive manner but yet he was still gentle enough that he didn't hurt anyone. Mato arrived at what looked like a small mechanic's corner. There was nothing but pieces of different types of electronics and vehicles all around. The bikes were small and weren't designed to handle the full-sized warrior. Mato didn't have a problem grabbing one of the two motorcycles that were available while Jay caught the other. He looked rather funny, like an adult on a child's toy, but he didn't let looks get in his way. Jay got on the bike and tried to keep pace with Mato. They now rode up the side ramps of the surrounding cliffs, then drove through hidden passageways with Mato in the lead. Jay kept track of the spies' locations via his armband personal assistant. The spies appeared as red dots, and he appeared as a single blue one that was fast approaching them.

Mato arrived first to the spot in the surrounding jungle where some trees and brush had been burned off. A space shuttle was parked in the middle of the clearing. It was explicitly colored to match the jungle background. The matte paint still made it stand out like a sour thumb but only when you knew to look for it. *These spies must have been planning this for a long time.* Jay was just moments behind Mato, but he didn't seem to be slowing down at all. This alerted the spies to what was going on. They turned and fired on Mato and Jay. Laser fire seared the air around them. Mato flipped over his motorcycle then laid on the ground to hide behind it. On the field, he could see Geeko running towards the space shuttle and entering it. He seemed to be trying to hide for safety as well. Jay's motorcycle roared past as he jumped off then fired upon it. The motorcycle exploded, rocking the otherwise peaceful and serene surrounding jungle. The Acolytes never stood a chance. They lay on the ground with some limbs missing, silent. The holographic field around them shuddered, and they no longer had the disguise of clones. One of the spies was large and bordering on fat, the other rail thin. Both middle-aged brown-skinned males looked nothing like the clones he was used to seeing. Mato was surprised at this development. He could see they wore armor and had holsters for their blasters on their sides. *This must have been what they kept grabbing for.*

Jay didn't slow down to look at the dead. He moved on and scanned for the artifact, finding it inside the shuttle. There he found the late model clone staring up at him. Geeko looked nervous. His face was filled with fear. Mato could see how panicked the boy was. Geeko looked to him for some type of approval, some type of common bond, an unspoken acknowledgment that it was us versus the outsider and didn't get it. Mato shrugged and shook his head in a move of denial.

"Give him what he wants," said Mato.

"Sure, anything you want man," Geeko agreed.

"Give me that special artifact you stole for The Acolytes, "demanded Jay.

"They were Acolytes?" Geeko responded. Geeko looked out the shuttle's window and saw the dead bodies. Even more shock and surprise was shown on his face. Mato didn't think it was possible at this point, but the late model was even more overwhelmed than he had been. Slowing backing away, Geeko reached in a sack he had been carrying with him and gave Jay the bronze encased circuit. The artifact.

Jay grabbed it and immediately raised a hand to his ear and called his team. "I got it. Ready the extraction, prepare to pacify the locals if we run into any trouble," said Jay.

"Eyota will be so happy that we returned the artifact. I bet I will be the captain of the honor guard now," said Mato

"I wouldn't bet on it kid," said Jay.

"Huh?"

"This thing is coming with me. I have a lady paying good money for it," said Jay.

"You can't do that! We will be defenseless when The Acolytes comes back," said Mato.

"What are you talking about Mato?" said Geeko.

"Whatever that thing is. It's how we defend ourselves when the rain starts," said Mato

"Oh!" said Geeko.

"You people will have to figure something else out because this is coming with me," said Jay. He waved the artifact at the young clones so they could see him secure it in his armor.

Mato balled his fist and gave a quick nod to Geeko. The late model knew precisely what he meant, and they sprang into action. Jay laughed and spun around, delivering a wicked backhand to Mato. Geeko jumped on Jay's back trying to reach and grab into the pocket where the artifact was secured in his armor. Jay was ready for this, and he reached back and flipped the child over him, tossing him a safe distance away. Jay knew his action would hurt, might even leave a bruise, but it wouldn't cause any permanent damage. They were just children after all. Mato hit his head against the shuttle walls. This made him lose consciousness immediately.

Jay picked up Mato then grabbed the defiant Geeko. He was heading back to the reservation when a beeping noise stopped him. *What is this? A bomb?* Blood rushed through his veins more rapidly, and he prepared for whatever awaited him after the noise stopped. A voice came on over the shuttle's communications.

"Elite Angel to Ghost… Elite Angel to Ghost… Come in. Was your mission a success?" A male voice asked.

Jay looked at Geeko and put his index finger over his mouth. "Shhhh"

Geeko grinned. His screaming hadn't affected the experienced mercenary, but he made Jay's eyes go wide when he opened his mouth.

"Don't do it," Jay whispered.

"Elite Angel to Ghost… Come in… Was the mission a success?" said the voice.

"The big brown guy stole the artifact from me, and he won't give it back!" shouted Geeko.

Jay's muscles grew hot and his blood boiled. Jay had to temper his rage.

"Who is this? Where is Ghost?" Jay stopped just short of a punch and gave a powerful downward slap making knocking Geeko out.

"Coming around for a second fire mission." Hissing sounds came from the central console as Jay shot it with his blaster.

Surveying the shuttle's storage room, Jay actually came into some luck. He found a small hovering trailer that he could use. He dropped the clones on the flat surface of the container and hooked it up to the remaining motorcycle. *A man on a small wheeled bike dragging a couple of knocking out clones. I'm going to max out and maybe even destroy this small engine. Well not like I need it for more than a couple of miles anyway.* The little engine whined as he drove off from the shuttle. Another beeping noise started in the background. This time there was no doubt in Jay's mind what it would signal. An explosion rocked the surrounding jungle, and a fire was started. He supposed the clones would put it out, eventually.

Slowing down to stop from running Eyota over, Jay dropped off the knocked-out clones. He looked at Eyota and said. "They are no soldiers, but they did well."

Eyota seemed to ignore the words and go directly into what was on his mind. "The Acolytes are coming back, and our defense grid is down. We are doomed. You must help us."

Jay looked at him. Gave him a 1000-yard stare. There wasn't much he could do. Jay debated in his mind on which way he should play this. How much did he owe Eyota, or should he leave him to his fate?

"What's going on?" Asked Claire on the secure line.

Humm guess I should go with the truth. It's not like these clones can stop me.

"The Acolytes had stolen the artifact, and it looks important. I bet that's what your defense grid is based on from the looks of it. But it's coming with me," said Jay.

Eyota's mouth dropped.

Claire huffed and puffed in his ear. "Is that what we came here for? To screw over the population?" Claire asked.

Jay's mouth was opening to respond when Eyota started his pleas. "Please, Please, help us. I'm a proud man but what would you have me do? Please."

Jay could hear his team start to complain at the same time over the intercom. He felt under attack. It was just verbal, but he felt like he was physically being assaulted on many fronts.

"If this is how Death's Witness does business I quit," said Claire.

"So, do I," said Ray

"Have fun completing this crap by yourself," said Bond.

"You STOP!! If you leave now, you won't get paid!" Jay shouted over the communication channel. It looked as though he was talking to himself while Eyota begged on his knees. Realizing he was having an effect on the situation Eyota groveled loudly, exaggerating his pleas so that they could be overheard by whoever was listening on the other end.

"No money you hear me," shouted Jay.

"We don't care," replied Ray.

"Cut the communication line, Claire," said Bond.

"Wait, wait. Give me a minute. I'll see what I can do," said Jay. What made Jay a good soldier and an even better mercenary was that he knew when it was time to back down from a fight. The years had taught him that.

Jay switched his communication channel off, looked at Eyota and said. "You can quit it now. You won. If a good team wasn't so hard to find in the galaxy, I would have just said fuck you both."

Eyota started to praise him with his gratitude.

"Keep it down this next call is going to be important," Jay continued.

"Yes, whatever you need," said Eyota.

"Jay to The Witness Eye, we need backup. Yes, this is an emergency."

Dozens of black ops and stealth ships arrived within the hour. They landed all around the reservation, soon dozens of intake ramps descended onto the ground as the various teams of Death's Witness welcomed the clone refugees onto their ships.

Jay looked up and around he saw the battleships of The Acolytes appear overhead. They descended from the heavens and were just barely visible. *They just want a better view.* "Pick up the pace," he yelled at the clones. He knew what was about to happen. Everyone did. The yelling, crying, screaming, it was all warranted. The air was getting dusty, and the scene was getting chaotic as the last clones picked up everything they had and moved quickly to the evacuation ships that Jay had ordered. *I'm not going to have a paycheck after this. Correction, the newbies, won't have a paycheck after this.* Jay thought, and this eased his mind a little bit. At least the debt from this ordeal would guarantee that his team won't be so easily able to quit on him again. At least not if they wanted to keep their heads. Jay was standing with his team in a very stoic pose. He looked over at them as they prepared one of the last ships. Their original ship, the on that they landed with. Jay told Bond "Get Eyota he comes with us."

"Yes Sir," said the young mercenary.

The sound of blasts raining down from the sky started.

"We have to go now!!" Jay ordered.

The ships closed their doors and departed, heading in the opposite direction from The Acolytes in the sky.

Bond reported back quickly. "Eyota is on our ship. So are those kids that helped you out."

"Helped me out? Oh, crap those little bastards," Jay replied. The sound of explosions started to echo from all around them.

"I think we have worn out our welcome," Claire joked.

All the younger members of the team laughed with her. The shuttles boomed as they lifted away from the planet, some were barely missed by the bombardment from above. The Death's Witness ships were cloaked, so they didn't have to worry about being directly targeted, but anyone could still get unlucky. That didn't happen this day, but it could.

It always could.

Claire was now piloting the ship. She was a good pilot, and her shorter stature didn't matter when it came to piloting so a pilot she was. "All the other ships are returning to The Witness Eye on Planet Cloverstone. I assume we are staying here to meet our client instead?" Claire asked.

"You assume correctly. I have a hot date with little miss Taryn. Orbit the planet, and we'll meet her at the original rendezvous," said Jay.

"Shouldn't we meet someone where else. This planet is crawling with Acolytes." Claire replied.

"They can't pierce this cloak or hers, so we don't have anything to worry about."

"If you say so," replied Claire.

Their ship orbited the planet from a small distance while The Acolytes bombed what remained of the reservation. The light shows from the ships created a beautiful scene of destruction. Green light rained down on the planet slowing turning what looked like a brown and green speck into nothingness.

A long cylinder ship with rotating platforms soon approached. Its cloak was good enough to mask it from Death's Witness' sensors, but an exception was already made so that they could see it on their instruments. The science vessel stood out among the warships Jay was used to seeing. This ship didn't have guns, it was painted a bright white color, and it had all types of box and gadgets attached to its outside. Jay looked at Claire, the young pilot, as she carefully aligned the two ships together. The vessels docked and for a moment the cloak would flicker while the ships synchronized. Everyone on board was silent during this wait. The Acolytes would turn and approach if they were detected.

"Several seconds have passed. No pings and no new movements from The Acolytes."

"Good, I don't want anyone interrupting my date," said Jay.

"What was that?" Taryn was already on board and standing right behind Jay. Jay's brown face grew flushed, and his teammates could tell that he was blushing. Lucky for him Taryn could not.

"Do you have what I paid you for?" She demanded.

"Yes, we do," said Jay as he handed over the artifact.

Eyota raised his hand in objection. He came rushing from the other side of the bridge.

"That is ours," Eyota stated.

Taryn moved her finger to the window of the ship, and she pointed towards The Acolytes. "It doesn't look like you will be needing it anymore." Taryn pulled her hand back to her while grabbing the artifact from Jay. She had jet black hair and matching skin tone. Her eyes were a very light, almost colorless mix of yellow and blue. As she turned away, her skin changed from the jet black to almost clear white.

"She is one of them. How can she even hear us?" Eyota stated.

"Not quite," Jay replied.

"The fact that she can change her skin tone like that freaks me out," whispered Bond.

Eyota nodded his head in agreement. Taryn didn't respond to their remarks as she seemed neither not to hear them or to be so desensitized to the reaction she got from people who were not her own race that she let them have this moment.

"Jay, are you coming with? We have many things to discuss as I track down the final few artifacts for my project," said Taryn.

"Coming," Jay replied. He turned and looked at Claire.

"You are in charge. Don't cock it up."

"I don't even have one," she replied.

Jay followed Taryn through the airlock and into her ship. She grabbed the artifact from her pocket and put it in a stasis field. She started the process of analyzing it in her computer system. She had a great many lining the walls and what looked like a chemical lab in the center.

"What I'm working on might just transform the galaxy. The Galactic Planetary League will be very pleased once they hear of our progress," said Taryn.

"I'm sure they will be. If there is anything you need my team is ready and able," said Jay as he sat down in one of the lab chairs and folded his arms on the top, spreading his legs on the sides. He tried to lift his head up and show his softer side. *Maybe if I showed less of a hard front, this lady would open up.* He thought. It appeared to be working. She kept talking about her project and how she represented the GPL. How grateful they were.

"You realize we might finally open the gate? We will know the origins of our Galaxy." She went on and on about this.

Remembering that he wanted to mix some business with pleasure Jay tried to change the subject.

"What do you need of my team now? We certainly can't help you with the science. My team is a bunch of smart cookies, but this is beyond us," said Jay.

Galactic Mandate: The Scream

"Right. Sorry, I can talk for hours about science. Let me get back to the matter at hand. You have already been paid for this job, but I have another for you. One that will cost a lot more I'm sure. We can discuss the details later but here is what I have now. Two more artifacts are missing, and one of them is in the silent territory. I will need your team to escort me back to League One, and the GPL can pay you for the new mission. I know the hazard fee will be substantial, but I have received word that money will be no hindrance. The GPL can pay you whatever you want, within reason."

Jay got out of his chair and stood up straight. *I can read a room and this ain't going in the direction I want it to.* "That is a lot to drop on me. You know I can't authorize a mission like that. I'll pass this up to my superiors and let you know what they say."

"If that is what needs to be done," said Taryn.

"You know this is a big ship for just one person to run. Do you need any help in the meantime? I'm sure it will take a couple of days to get a decision. The Acolytes will be gone by then, and we will just be out here alone."

"As tempting as it would be to have help around the lab and run more experiments. I'm needed on League One. Set the course at once. My zero drive will slave to yours so we can arrive at the same time. Off with you now," said Taryn.

Jay returned to his own ship, had Claire plot the course, and they started the zero-drive countdown. Both ships were synchronized, so the countdowns were duplicated across both.

"Five, four, three, two, one," said the ship's computer, and they were off. They moved to do their maintenance tasks while they traveled.

"Bond how many clones do we have on board?" asked Jay.

"Way too many," he responded.

"Can I get an exact count please?"

"Roughly a hundred. sixty males and forty females about," said, Bond.

"I guess that is close enough," replied Jay.

Gravity shifted, and Jay was knocked off of his feet. Everything the wasn't bolted down went flying. Complaints started coming in from the clones in the decks below while Jay got on his communicator.

"What was that?"

"We hit an interdiction field. They pulled us out of zero space early, "Claire responded.

"I thought that was impossible."

"I don't know, ask your girlfriend about the science. We got a problem right now. I'll need you to get up here."

Jay got back on his feet and rushed to the head of the ship. He looked out the window and uttered "Oh god." Jay's eyes surveyed the area surrounding the ship. Large barely painted and hastily put together ships hovered above them. They showed the symbols of space pirates, and there were other disabled ships belonging to Death's Witness.

"What do we do?" Claire asked.

"We should have quit," said Bond.

"Where is Taryn's ship. Did she make it through?" asked Jay.

Claire shook her head and said, "she's over there."

Taryn's science vessel was rotating on its center axis spinning towards the pirate ships at a slow pace. Blue lights emerged from the mess of the pirate carriers. Very small fighter and tug ships. They were going to be pulled in and pillaged.

"Grab your weapons. If we go down. We go down swinging," said Jay.

"We can't do that we have one hundred civilians on board," said Bond.

"Oh, now you know how to give exact numbers," said Jay.

"I didn't forfeit my pay just so I could watch the clones die here rather than back there," said Claire.

"We have to stand down, Boss, for the sake of the clones," said Bond.

"Great, just, great. Tell me did you two plan to do any fighting when you signed up for this mission or was it always surrendering at the first sign of trouble?" asked Jay.

"That's not fair," said Bond

"It never will be kid," said Jay.

They were dragged into the carriers. Everyone was walked out of Death's Witness' shuttle with their hands on their head. Many of the clones had been wounded when the ship had come to a sudden stop. The wounds would not be treated. Not by the Pirates. They seem to sort the clones by physical ability, then next by gender. They put everyone they could find into cages. Anyone who slowed down the pirates got a shock collar installed around their necks. The pirates enjoyed watching people grab for their collar as the electricity flowed through them.

"It's amazing how fast people can heal when they have some motivation," said a pirate as he shocked some wayward clones.

Jay and his team left the ship last. They seemed to look around at each other. Jay still yearned to fight but he looked at their faces, and he confirmed that his younger team members didn't have the will for it. With his hands on his head, he passed by cages in the dark docking bay. Already filled with clones and the team members from the other ships, they yelled out at him. They asked him to do something. Jay just winked and hollered back.

"This won't last long just you wait."

Pirate ran at him with shock sticks. They must have figured he was too big or too tough to put a collar on. Jay yelled out in agony as he was electrocuted from three different sides. Jay fell to his knees. Looking behind him, he could see Taryn was being brought on board as well. The pirates took her from the comfort of her science vessel and brought her directly to the docking bay. She already had a shock collar on herself, and she nervously switched her skin color from white to black and back again.

"She must be really nervous," said a pirate.

"Don't worry we won't hurt ya," said another.

"Ok, maybe just a little," said a third. The pirates laughed.

"What is going on?" Mato asked Jay. He was being held in a cage directly in front of where Jay was lying on the ground. Eyota was in the cage right behind him, his fate now so more than ever tied with the clones. Jay was getting up after being shocked so many times.

"You are the fighter huh?" Jay asked.

"No talking to the produce," said one of the pirates.

"They are people," said Taryn.

The pirates looked back in shock. They stood quietly while their leader ruffled through the crowd to see what all the silence was about.

"Who could make all my men finally shut up? Even I can't do that," came a lady's voice from the back of the room. The Pirates moved out of her way as she came closer.

"It can't be," Jay muttered.

"Long time no see," exclaimed CJ. "Yes, it's me. I have a new gig. You know, you should have stuck with the pirating now, don't ya?" she continued. She wore a bright yellow dress the contrasted against her black leggings and draped mustard and black cape.

"So, you are the head of The Quantum Pirates?" Jay asked.

CJ raised her arms, and her scepter and rotated slowly. "Do you see anyone else giving the orders? If you do, let me know I'll bring Jax out to gut them."

The pirates hooted and howled in support.

"What have you done with him?" Jay asked.

"Oh, that is right. You haven't been here since then, have you. Come with me," she motioned for the mercenaries to come and follow her. Jay tapped his collar, and CJ looked at it and gave a slight frown. "Don't think I'm going to take that off for one second."

"Shit, it was worth a try," said Jay. The Pirates moved their shock batons towards Taryn in a slow and sinister approach. "She is with me," exclaimed Jay.

CJ nodded in Taryn's direction. The pirates backed off. CJ nodded again, and the pirates released her from her collar. Jay gave a confused look, and CJ responded.

"What? I treat my ladies better than you do."

Jay rolled his eyes and was interrupted by a slight shock.

"I won't tolerate any disrespect. Not anymore," CJ warned.

CJ turned around and strutted down the messy halls of the ship, taking every chance to show Jay her new power. She ordered underlings. She walked in the middle of crowds and pushed those who didn't notice her approach to the side. The pirates were as thin and frail as they were cruel. Each one looked malnourished, but CJ didn't look like she missed a meal. Her hair was in its usual long braid as she led them to a loft above a cargo bay that held mostly junk fighters. Jay couldn't tell which were used for parts and which ones worked. It was all a twisted mess of brown metal below them. *Defeated by a bunch of low lives who can't even keep a cargo bay clean. How the mighty have fallen.*

Galactic Mandate: The Scream

Once CJ opened the doors to the small enclosed room overlooking the docking bay, Jay's eyes grew wide. Jax was lying in a cryo-pod that was upright slanted against the wall. He had a permanent look of rage on his frozen face. Mouth open, Jay looked to CJ for an explanation. Bond interrupted the eye contact with a question.

"Isn't that your famous teammate? I think I recognize him from pictures back at the EYE," Bond blurted out.

"Yes, kid, that's Jax. And you better have an explanation for this," said Jay

"What did I say about the disrespect?" rebutted CJ. She turned on the shock collar, and Jay screamed. "Watch, I want you to know what happens to Jay. This is your destiny if you stay with him." Jay's team was helpless to resist as they watched him claw at his neck trying to get the torture device off of him.

"You want to know what happened? Well, I will tell you. Jax, my chocolate man of love, he took a liking to the drugs we were peddling. This was about the time you got out Jay. In fact, I think this is your fault. Once you left, there was no one to stop him from doing drugs all night. I wasn't complaining because the drugs made him rock hard in mind and body. He could last all night. How could a lady complain about that? Do you understand what I am saying, my new recruits?" CJ stopped her story and slowly turned down Jay's shock collar.

He no longer screamed, and she was happy to have his full attention now. With his eyes locked on her, she moved to the shell of the cryo-pod, gyrated and moaned in an exaggerated manner. When everyone tried to look away, she activated the shock collar.

"Eyes on me!" she demanded.

"Where was I? I was talking about fucking! And good. Jax didn't need the drugs for that, but it's not like we are running a convent. He pillaged liked no other, and he took what I wanted from any and everyone. He couldn't be stopped, except by himself and his body. The drugs, they poisoned his brain, and now his brain poisons his body. I have to keep him in cryo, or he would rip my head off along with everyone in this room. The Rage took him. Like it will take you, Jay. Hehe," CJ giggled menacingly.

She knew she had all the power and was drunk off the control she exerted at this moment. "Go now," CJ commanded.

***

...Back at the cage...

"How are we going to get out of this?" asked Claire.

"We should have just quit," said Bond. They were all locked in a makeshift cage directly below CJ. They were able to look up at her and see her through the floor of her room. CJ had the room above custom made to have a clear floor when she wanted it to. She was able to change it from transparent to opaque on command. She kept a watchful eye on Jay's crew. A bunch of pirates rushed in the room, and they seemed to be in a panic. They pointed and showed CJ displays of what looked to be a map of the ship. It showed all the locations of the prisoners. CJ changed the floor to opaque before Jay, and his team could see a readout of the critical systems.

Taryn looked around the cage and put her arms up.

"I thought I paid you enough to avoid inconveniences such as this."

"We are just running into to some bad luck, that is all."

"What is this history that you two have? Is this how your ex-girlfriends end up?" Taryn asked.

"Low blow," said Jay.

"This is no time to talk about ex-girlfriends and who dated who. How in the hell are we going to get out of this?" said Claire.

"Yeah, aren't you a scientist Taryn? Can't help you get us out of these shock collars?" Bond asked.

"Yes, and how do you expect me to do that? Use my magic science powers to think really hard and unlock the collars? I need tools, and we don't have any here. But even if I did, what are we going to do then? I haven't heard a plan from any of you," Taryn replied.

"You can leave that up to me. I'll take care of the pirates then we can be on our way," said Jay.

"I doubt it," said Taryn.

"Excuse me?"

Galactic Mandate: The Scream

"I'm not doing anything until we have a plan," said Taryn.

"How did the pirates find us anyway? We were in zero space, that is supposed to be impossible," said Bond.

"Humm that is a good question. I didn't think you were capable of such thought," said Taryn

"Don't talk to him that way," said Claire.

"Yes, let me use simple words for the present company. The technology to pull ships out of zero space shouldn't exist. It's beyond anything in the galaxy. I've actually been pondering how the pirates did it. I haven't seen anyone on board with the technical skills. I could unlock the collars, but I think we need to stay a while until I figure out how they did it. Besides the technology might help my project," said Taryn.

"What? Unlock us now!" said Bond.

"Cool it, team," said Jay.

"Don't give us orders. You lost control when they put a collar on you. Don't scream and get us all shocked," rebutted Claire.

"That is that problem with you young kids playing soldier. When I was your age, I was neck deep in enemy kills. You have no heart, no gumption. A wet sock is more useful than you and Bond."

"You're a terrible leader trying to use brute force with every fight is why we are stuck in here," replied Claire.

"The fact that you never fight is why we are here," said Jay.

"How are we having this conversation right now? The pirates should have shocked us by now," said Bond.

"You do have a point," said Jay.

Just then they were interrupted by sounds of screaming and panic from above. The argument had escalated, and now it spilled out. A pirate, a smaller male, was thrown from the room and landed on his back. He groaned, and he rolled on his side trying to lessen the pain. CJ yelled.

"What do you mean there is a problem with the zero drive? Where the hell are we going to find someone to fix it out here? We are in the middle of nowhere."

"We don't know. There isn't anyone on board with the technical skills to fix it. We are doomed I tell you."

"Abandon ship," said another.

"The hell we are! Not after the haul we just captured. Midnight is going to pay a fortune for this. She loves selling clones on the black market. You don't fix it, you don't eat. And if I catch you running, I'm aiming to blow you out of the sky," yelled CJ.

"Seem there is a need for my skills here," Taryn said as she smiled.

Jay frowned. He hated his options, but he knew what he had to calm down. He exhaled a breath then yelled upwards at the metal bridge where the argument was taking place.

"Hey!"

CJ moved her fingers to the remote trigger for the shock collars and gave them a glance. "It better be important, or I will show you what these collars can really do."

"Taryn. She can solve your problem," said Jay.

CJ selected the collars of Taryn, Bond, and Claire. *Test me I have a surprise for you if you are wasting my time.* CJ thought. She moved her finger away from the shock button and moved it lower hovering over a different button that was bright red.

"How so?" CJ responded.

"She is the lead scientist for the GPL. Fixing your zero drive should be child's play."

"What a lucky break. See, aren't you happy I captured you?" said CJ.

"If you don't fix the zero drive, we all die. Do you understand that?" explained a man who seemed to be the lead mechanic for the Quantum Pirates.

"No need to explain the repercussions to me," said Taryn.

Taryn was rushed to the Engine Room. She was confronted by a drive that was sparking and venting excess electricity across the room. She looked around and saw the controls. Taryn moved to the control panel.

She input a quick override to admin, "Do you need the passwords?" said the head mechanic.

"I know the designer of this drive, so, umm, no. Get out of my way, and I will have this fixed in a couple minutes," boasted Taryn.

The lighting of the room turned to red as a harsh beeping came from the panel.

"You are going to kill us," said the mechanic.

Galactic Mandate: The Scream

"Stop panicking, this is under control," Taryn said, trying and failing to ease the mechanic's fear. She knew computers, science, even basic mechanics, but people they always confused her. They were unpredictable, and she didn't like that.

"Move out the way," she finally stated.

The mechanic objected, but he seemed so overwhelmed there was nothing he could do to resist. The repair was beyond him, and he knew that.

Taryn diagnosed the problem in what she thought was record time. If only the competition shows could see her now. She always dreamed of competing with her fellow scientists on the holo-networks, but she could never find someone that could give her a challenge. At least not on this side of the galaxy. The diagnostic reported a simple error. The circuits were fluctuating too much and caused the zero drive to be out of synch. All she had to do was calculate the drive rotation factoring in cosmic radiation and the phase of the zero drive's root factors. She put in the calibrations and watched as the drive got worse. It fizzed and popped, striking out and killing the head mechanic instantly. Her pirate guards moved away. They kept a close eye like that of spectators at a sports event, but they now kept their distance.

That should have worked. I don't understand, my calculations were perfect. She thought. Then she looked up and saw the rotating artifact. It spun in an aftermarket attachment to the zero drive. Standing directly at eye level, it had two forks, one reaching out from the ceiling and one from a platform on the floor, and in the middle was an artifact that looked exactly like that one handed to her by Jay. *That's it. That is how they pulled us from zero space and why the ship is in trouble now. I have to get that artifact.* Taryn typed in the calibrations using her prior knowledge from studying similar artifacts and corrected her previous mistakes. *I have to get my hands on that artifact! Its abilities are so unique. It's not like any of the others that I have seen.*

"I found the missing artifact. All by myself. I hope Jay is ready to negotiate a discount." She smiled.

***

He awoke 96 from the cryo chamber.

"I hope this experiment has better results than the last," Dr. Don said to himself. *It's time for something new.*

"Where am I?" 96 asked.

"You are in my lab," the doctor replied.

"Where is my crew? Where are my friends?"

"Well, I assume they have been dead for a while," said Dr. Don.

It took 96 a while to notice the peculiarity of the situation around him. The doctor in front of him had black skin. He was a lanky man with a strange skin-tight lab coat. He didn't really speak much, he actually waved his hands, and a device on his neck spoke out. It translated his hand motions into language that 96 could understand. It even spoke to him in his native accent. 96 was impressed. He didn't remember how he got here. He didn't remember much, just that he had been on Emerton and somehow, he was here. His head was fuzzy from the cryo. He thought he must have spent time in a defective pod because it couldn't be like this for everyone. It was nothing like those commercials on the holo-network made it seem.

"How do you feel?" The doctor signed.

"Groggy, and it's hard to remember things," 96 replied.

"That is to be expected. I want you to do something for me," signed the doctor.

"Ok."

96 was suspicious and knew that he was not in his element. He wanted to see how this played out and what was really going on before he figured out how to get out of this lab and get back to his friends. The doctor had to be lying. After all the strange and unique things he had seen in this galaxy, a doctor doing some kind of illegal experiment was almost mundane. *I'll just consider this my checkup. I haven't actually seen a doctor since I was with the chancellor, and I now know that they did not have my best interest at heart, although it's not like this guy has something better planned for me.*

"I want you to focus on the light." There were some bright lights in the middle of the room. They shined in his eyes, and he tried to shy away from them.

"Don't do that. Confront the lights and try to draw energy from them." 96 stood up and puffed his chest out at the light in the center of the room. The was nothing unusual about the light, just the strange doctor and the strange request from him.

"Now what?" 96 asked.

"Try to draw energy from the light," said the doctor.

"How am I going to do that?"

"Just try."

96 puffed his chest out and stood directly under the light. He stared straight into it and burned his retina. He could barely see, but nothing happened.

"What are you trying to do with this?" 96 asked.

"Just focus," commanded the doctor.

96 did as he was instructed and held his pose for a while, losing tension in his muscles and then relaxing for a bit only to get yelled at to focus harder.

"This is ridiculous. Give me a spaceship and let me be on my way. I thank you for thawing me out, but I must get going. I have a crew to look after."

"That gives me an idea," the doctor reached under a large steel table for a hose that was connected to the floor.

Freezing air came spewing out . It chilled 96, and he put his hands up to block the cold. His body reached for the energy that was provided under that light and first his skin went white from the cold making the doctor react with a smile. 96 felt his body reach out and try to grab and suck in the light that was now the only source of energy in the room. He felt his skin react again and go black. 96 felt a special tingling a sensation around his tattoo as it reacted differently from the stimulus. It seemed to invert, and its edges burned.

"Yes, yes. I have done it. With the help of this artifact. I have created the first convert to our kind," said Doctor Don. He bobbed his head from side to side in a sort of celebration. His hair froze from the cold air hose that he had let loose in the room. 96 stared at his hand and looked around in amazement.

"What have you given me?"

96 didn't know what these new abilities would bring, but he was happy for it.

***

The pirate was about to put the collar back on Taryn when CJ came down from her room to personally thank her.

"Thank you, you have saved the Quantum Pirates, we owe you our lives. Which isn't worth much."

The pirates around her laughed, a genuine laughter that Taryn didn't understand. *Why giggle at having so little to offer society?* She thought.

"As a token of my gratitude, I'm letting you go to any pleasure room once we get to Skymark. On me," said CJ.

"I couldn't accept something like that. I could lose my position in the GPL if I were caught in one of those rooms," said Taryn.

"Please, you will be the only one in the GPL who hasn't been caught in one. These dignitaries will never accept you as one their own unless you have some skeletons in your closets to share," said CJ.

"I'd rather not," said Taryn.

"If you are worried about your position, I say you should be worried about your head. Not accepting a pirate's generosity who has been known to be deadly. "

"Do they have a quite pleasure room where I can get caught up on my work?" asked Taryn.

"Then don't get a room by me," said CJ, then she continued. This caused another round of laughter," "It's a VIP pleasure room. They'll do whatever you want."

"Let me inform my team of the new arrangements," said Taryn

"I have specials plans for Jay. Trust me, if you hired him, you should look for new help," said CJ.

They were in earshot of Jay and his team as they stared on from their cage. Claire and Bond looked up, and they pulled on their collars.

Jay looked back and whispered. "This is just a setback."

"The zero drive is fixed," CJ stated.

"Computers are saying 100%," said one of the pirate leaders.

"How do we know she didn't sabotage it?" said another.

"That is a good question. We don't, but I can show her what it means to mess with us. There are riches there are spoils if you are our friends. We will make sure you have all the wrong things that life can offer. And if you are our enemies," CJ locked eyes with Claire she stared at Jay in the cage and pressed the button she had been dying to press for a while. Blades came out of the shock collar Claire was wearing, chopping her head off cleanly. Blood spurted out from the neck and drained on the floor from her lifeless head that bounced on the floor of the cage.

Jay muttered a damn and reacted with a balled fist. "Bond. This is why you fight." He muttered.

Bond was yelling hysterically making a combination of cries and screams. He grabbed the head from the floor and screamed into it. "What have you done?" he asked repeatedly.

Jay sat down and let his head rest on the cell bars. *That won't be me. Because I fight.*

Taryn looked away and never looked at the cage again. She closed her eyes and tried to remember her formulas and cast her mind back to what seemed like just a couple of minutes ago. Thinking about all the lives she saved. How the clones, her team, and the pirates were all still alive because of her. She tried not to think about Claire. The shocked look that was stuck on her severed head.

"Trust me, girl, I did you a favor. Running with Jay was never a smart idea. If we land anywhere near the GPL, if we find out you sabotage the zero drive, if we find out you worked against us in any way. You are next," said CJ.

"I have no intention of sabotaging you. That is not something I would do," said Taryn.

"Off we go," said CJ waving her left hand in the air and making a circle with it. The coordinates were programmed in. The lead mechanic asked for an hour or so make the necessary preparation for zero drive.

"Don't forget to make sure the clones are ready. I don't want my new merchandise to be damaged before we get there." CJ commanded.

Chapter 9

The clones were herded into new cells. The conditions on the station were a slight upgrade from the makeshift pirate ship prison. The new confinements were clean and had proper facilities to house such a number of clones. They also had medical facilities, and while overwhelmed by the sheer number of prisoners, they made an effort to see every injured clone they could. This wasn't done out of some effort of goodwill. Clones that were healthy were much more valuable than clones that were sick and injured. Sick clones even presented a risk to the patron's health. The Daydream was a beautiful station and had a reputation to keep.

CJ let Taryn pick a pleasure room and had her men escort her to it. They allowed her to have some privacy but kept a watchful eye over the entrance so she wouldn't escape. Taryn's collar was removed and more and more she was treated as if she were pirate. Taryn felt disgusted at the thought of joining this ragtag group of low-lives. She wondered if they truly knew who she was and how much value she brought.

"These people are idiots. They have no idea of my value. I'm worth three whole cruisers filled with pirates. Even then they couldn't match my brain power," Taryn smiled and giggled to herself.

With Taryn preoccupied, CJ collected Jay and what remained of his team along with Eyota who requested a single clone come with him, Mato.

"I need to bring you all to see our Leader. He will be happy to see you, especially you, Jay," said CJ.

Jay grimaced. He was bound in magnetic cuffs, and his collar was still on him. Bond, Eyota, and Mato were all bound in the same manner. They were led in a chain gang past halls and halls of pleasure rooms until they reached the main elevator. This elevator took them into the center of the space station. Bond and Mato's eyes went wide. The main floor was a sight to behold. Surrounded by glass on all sides, the level was one large room with beds at every axis and comforting rugs. Jay's face showed a look of concern and confusion. His eyes went slightly wide while he looked at the figure in the middle of the room.

Jay thought the central figure looked familiar but couldn't place it. Standing before him in some kind of white leggings and black shirt and armor that he definitely recognized but was made smaller and more feminine than he remembered. It now had curves where it should be straight but the battle scars and coloring combinations, he definitely recognized them. There was only one person in the Galaxy to whom it belonged. The person in front of him had extremely dark skin that was exposed on her arms, and she wore white chalk on her face. "That's Extra's armor, what have you done with him," said Jay.

"I'm here. I decided this form would work better in my current profession," said Midnight.

"You were always an interesting one," Jay said.

"I see you have met my pirates." She waved her hand towards the wide window on the far wall from the elevator. From the middle of the space station, you could see all the ships that were docked and all the approaching and disembarking ships that were around. It made an enjoyable sight. Midnight could see everything that a station owner needed to see in this one place.

"Eyota is it?" said Midnight. "You are free to go. For a small rescue fee of course."

The guards came around, and he was unhooked from his restraints, and the collar was removed. CJ smiled at the man.

"I'm not going anywhere without the clones." Eyota resisted.

She ignored him. "You can stay. It will be full price. No need to worry, we already have your accounts for billing. Seems like one of your secretaries is a little overzealous. She felt obligated to help the little madam from the pleasure station who hadn't been paid. Do you see Jay? This form has its advantages," said Midnight.

"Seems to suit you better. You never were a great soldier. You could never take a man's life from up close and personal, you had to hide and shoot him from afar," said Jay.

CJ zapped him but was stopped by Midnight.

"It's ok. We have some things to settle," said Midnight. CJ moved her finger off of the button for the electric control. "He can speak his mind to me. After all, I owe that respect to my old teammate."

Jay looked up once the pain was stopped "You are pathetic. This form. This station is nothing, and I'm going to destroy it all," said Jay.

"Watch it. You can disrespect my time in the service all you want but once you threaten my business that's when things become fatal." Midnight took a blaster from a rack of them that were displayed by her bed and pointed it at Jay's head.

CJ heard a buzzing in her communication device, followed by another. She touched it and heard Taryn's voice.

"You said I can get whatever I wanted in the pleasure room, right?" said Taryn.

"What! How are you on this channel?" said CJ.

"Genius scientist remember? Can I get Jay in my room for a night of fun or not?"

CJ looked at Jay who was as defiant as ever. His short hair was glistening with sweat as he stared down the barrel of Midnight's blaster. CJ walked over to Midnight and tapped her on the shoulder.

"This one is requested upstairs," whispered CJ.

"You're in luck. The customer is always right, so you're going upstairs," announced Midnight. She looked at her guards and gave a quick nod. They picked Jay up and moved him back to the elevator.

"What are we going to do with the clone?" Asked CJ.

"He seemed to be special to Eyota. Drop him off in his room and be done with this crowd," said Midnight.

"That leaves the last member of Death's Witness left," said CJ.

"Oh him. He stays with me. I have a fun use for him."

Chapter 10

"Do you like my body, Bond?" Midnight asked as she slowly removed her old armor, releasing a pseudo-military command jacket. It was black and white like the other symbols around the space station. Bond could see the reflection of the white face outline on her back against the glass of the space station. She removed more and more clothing. She approached Bond, and she caressed his face with her hands. Soon, she was just in her bra and a set of panties. She encroached on his personal space. He wanted to shy away. A range of emotions were running through Bond, from attraction and lust to repulsion and the underlying urge to break free.

Bond thought about how he could rush to the rack of guns and take some of the elevator guards down, all he needed to do was break free of the shackles and his collar. The collar would be the hardest part. Due to its remote control, he would have to live in constant fear that they could activate it at any time during his escape. He didn't want to lose his head, but being someone's plaything was not how he wanted to end up. No matter what form they took or how attractive they currently were, Bond didn't want to end up in this position.

Bond looked back at the door guard then at the Midnight. He then felt and rubbed the collar on his neck. Maybe there was a more diplomatic way to do this, he thought. Midnight already seemed to be taking a liking to him, so he could use that to his advantage. Maybe if I play along, I can find a release for the collar, it's nothing but freedom from there.

"Crawl to me," demanded Midnight. She had picked up a small electro whip and a bag. What she planned to do with the items, Bond didn't want to find out, but he decided playing along would be the best course of action for right now. *I must gain her trust, then when she is distracted, I can make my escape.* Midnight backed away and whipped the ground, demanded Bond come closer to her.

Bond crawled towards her and kept his head down, trying to avoid eye contact.

"Do it again, but slower. People want to see you. This needs to last at least twenty to thirty minutes, and if you just try to rush to get through it, I can't sell the Holovid. And pretend like you are enjoying it," said Midnight.

"OK," said Bond.

"Not OK, I need you to say, 'Yes Madam.'"

Midnight hit him with the whip. He winced, trying not to admit that it hurt.

"That's more like it. Had to make it fun. And if you behave, I'll have a reward for your good behavior." As Midnight was speaking, Bond looked around and saw that without him noticing, three different cameramen had triangulated around them and were getting views of Midnight and him as they interacted. They made sure to get the stars in the background. Oddly, Bond thought about how the stars and the pirate ships would make good scenery for a Holovid. It certainly must be better than the low-quality recruitment vid that he viewed when joining Death's Witness. He should have known that anything made that quick and cheap wouldn't be good for him. They told him how he would see the Galaxy, make fast money, and do good. Get out of his backwater world and make a difference in the galaxy. *I should have been careful what I wished for.*

She had him move to different positions and follow her around the bed in the room. Midnight kept mentioning how excited she was and how he would be rewarded. Bond was starting to think this could just be a shameful section in his life that he would never mention or talk about. *I can get through this. One Holovid shouldn't be that popular. People will forget as soon as the next one comes out anyway. The type of people who are watching this won't be watching to memorize who they saw.* It came time for him to crawl on the bed.

"It's time for the main event," said Midnight. Bond lay down, then closed his eyes. Expecting to be introduced to some weird or new fetish he'd never heard of, he lay there waiting for his next command. "Open your eyes. I want you awake for this."

Galactic Mandate: The Scream

Opening them, he looked at the rather plain metallic ceiling. It had random images and symbols he didn't recognize appear and disappear across it. Still waiting for his next instruction, he lifted his head just a little to see what was occurring in the room around him. Midnight took this as an opportunity and covered his head with the plastic bag she had been carrying around. It was sucked in by the collar, creating an airtight seal. He thrashed and reached for space that used to be present in the collar, but it had shrunk and formed to his neck. The camera shined lights in his eyes as he waved his arms and lashed out at Midnight. He moved his body upright and shook his hands into broad slaps that connected with nothing but air. He felt Midnight's soft body grab him from behind him and wrestle him to the ground, stopping his last tantrum and the last chance of survival before he took the last breath. He fell to the floor, lifeless.

"Excellent video, Midnight," said the nearest cameraman as he turned his hovering camera off. It whooshed back into his hand. "You will finally take the top spot on the underground network with this one, I guarantee."

"I'm betting one million copies sold," said another.

"This better meet your guarantees, or you're taking his place next time," replied Midnight.

"No, no need for that. We can use the clones for your next material."

"Yes."

"The great thing about them is we can pretend it's the same person. People will wonder how you bring them back each time," the first cameraman said. "And we will always have one to introduce to people in case they claim it's a fake video."

"Think of the profits, we can rent them out in the pleasure rooms. Sleep with a Holovid star, and it doesn't cost a fortune." Midnight rubbed her chin. "I like the idea of that. Get them prepared. A man and a woman. I want them to start production as soon as this Holovid hits. No breaks, we have money to make."

Chapter 11

Jay was shoved into the suite. They left him shackled and removed his clothes. He just had on a pair of white undergarments over his naked brown skin. Taryn, trying to remain composed, slowly moved toward him.

"Can we get some privacy?" she asked.

CJ and her escort of pirates left the room. CJ turned before leaving through the door. "Don't have too much fun." Holding up the remote, she moved her figure to the fatal button. Jay's name was clearly visible at the label above the button that said terminate.

"You said I could have anything," said Taryn. CJ made a grunting noise and moved on.

"She hasn't changed a bit," Jay stated.

"I can see why you have gone your separate ways," Taryn replied.

Jay looked up and noticed she was already removing a panel from his collar and had disabled his magcuffs.

"Sorry to burst your bubble but sex is not why I want you here. We are going to take over a ship and continue the project."

"Not if I don't get paid," said Jay as the door to the suite's bedroom slid open behind him.

Taryn dropped her tools and stared into his eye. "Maybe you are only good for some quick pleasure. I'm sure you can figure a way out of that collar by yourself. You and CJ seemed to be having so much fun, I would hate to interrupt," said Taryn.

Eyota coughed in a pronounced manner as he emerged from hiding, trying to draw the attention away from what he may have thought was a very private moment. "If payment is what you need. I can get it to you."

Jay crumbled his lips and nodded.

Taryn picked her tools back up and went back to work on his collar. "Keep still. If I mess this up, I could trigger the kill switch."

"I guess my life is in your hands," said Jay.

"Taryn was able to contact the GPL. Unfortunately, they aren't sending any rescue party. We are on our own," said Eyota.

"That's not all. We have to capture a pirate ship and go to Silent Space ourselves. I must find a way to convince them to give me the last artifact that I need for my Portal Project. The successful completion is almost at hand. You are going to be a part of history. With these artifacts we are going to open up new galaxies for exploration," bragged Taryn.

"Maybe one where I and the clones can live in peace," said Eyota.

"You wouldn't be rich in such a place. Are you sure you could handle that?" said Jay.

"Let me worry about that."

"We don't have enough manpower. We need more than just me, you and the rich guy, Taryn," said Jay.

"I can help," Mato chimed in from the bedroom. "I want to fight."

"This ain't schoolyard scraping," said Jay.

"Neither is what they are going to do to me if I stay here," was the reply.

"You got a point there."

"Done," said Taryn. The collar device opened up and fell to the floor. "We don't have much time now. I'm sure it alerted the pirates that something is wrong."

Jay got up and didn't bother to get dressed. He looked around and frowned. "Do we have any weapons?"

Eyota revealed powerful blasters that were shiny and chrome, along with additional battery packs.

"Wow, where did you get those things?"

"I'm rich remember. I just bought them. Guess being in an illegal space station has its perks," said Eyota. He threw a long rifle to Jay and gave Taryn a pistol. She rejected it and gave it to Mato instead. Eyota had a pistol as well, even though he seemed to be offended by the weapon's bold straight lines and chrome finish. "They wouldn't let me out of the store unless I got the top model. Something plain would have been better."

He frowned at the sight of Mato holding the pistol. He took him to the side and lowered his voice so only the young clone could hear him.

"Are you sure about this? I can't protect you from this world. If you leave with them you will be on your own," said Eyota.

"I want to fight for my clone brothers and sisters. No one else will," said Mato.

"I know you will. Of all of us, you have become the greatest warrior. Do us proud. I must stay here and look after the clones that I can," said Eyota.

Eyota showed Mato how to prime the weapon and get it battle ready.

"This is how most blasters work. Point it and shoot at the person you want to kill and only point it at someone if you want to kill them. Don't play with it. It's not a toy," Eyota warned.

"I understand," said Mato.

"Go," said Eyota.

Jay looked over the new recruit and thought about how much training he would need just to fight with his secretary back at the Eye.

"I guess this will have to do," Jay mumbled to himself.

Jay, Mato, and Taryn lined up at the door ready for Jay to start the assault.

"Wait.......Jay, we have some extra clothes in the suite. Come to put something on before you set out on your mission," said Eyota.

"No thanks, if the pirates didn't want to see my dick, they shouldn't have taken my clothes."

Jay overcharged his rifle. Taking the extra battery pack, he pointed the gun down and held the battery facing the door. Mato and Taryn stared at the nearly naked man and stood back.

"I'll save your butt another day," Mato whispered to Eyota.

The Battery pack glowed from the feedback. It was red hot and smoldering.

"A little trick I learned from some desperate followers of Darkness. They sure can fight when their backs are against the walls."

"I thought they were your allies," Said Taryn.

Jay smirked and grunted a little. "Only when the money is right," he replied.

Galactic Mandate: The Scream

Jay popped out the battery, projecting it into the door like a grenade. It exploded, creating a quick and fast black cloud filling the room with dust. Jay slammed an extra Battery pack into the shiny rifle and looked back.

"It's gone time fuckers."

Rushing into the hallway, the emergency lights were already flashing and alarms blaring. The explosion was enough to knock the guards that were near unconscious. Jay pointed his rifle down at their prone bodies and shot their heads off.

"These fuckers had too much fun from me. Don't show any mercy kid," he yelled back at Mato.

Three pirates ran down the hallway towards them. Jay squatted and started blasting away. Taryn and Mato followed close behind. Mostly hiding behind Jay, Mato took shots of opportunity, his inexperience on prominent display. Mato waited for a chance to get in close so he could do what he did best and solid punch and kick the enemy. He had not yet had his chance.

The first three pirates were shredded by the hail of fire coming from Jay's rifle. They moved down the hall and slowly made their way to the elevators. Mato tried to make a dash for the open door. Jay grabbed his shoulder and pulled him in close. Mato was in too much shock to react to the situation. He was being held by a muscular soldier who stood naked except for a thin piece of underwear.

"Don't go in there; it's a trap."

Just as Jay spoke, the elevator lost control. It went up and down turning into a dangerous saw-like device.

"Thanks," said Mato as he pulled away.

Taryn now gave an order. "Follow me. I downloaded the layout. As usual, I am the most prepared."

They ran down another hall, encountering more pirates. The pirates looked desperate and rushed. They didn't aim correctly and were easy for Jay to deal with. Mato had to focus with every pull of his trigger. The shooting didn't come so easily for him, and he wanted to fight now, but he also wanted to live to see another fight. Jay looked over his shoulder to see the young clone covering their rear. He held his chrome pistol up to his eye line and was dedicated to every shot.

"Here," said Jay as he tossed him another blaster.

This was a ragged and rugged looking thing that was obviously pulled from a pirate. Xs and Os were etched across its small brown frame. It had exposed cooling and a trigger that took more force than a normal gun. Mato grabbed it and fired with his dominant hand. It felt better; it resisted more and made him feel powerful.

A pair of pirates turned the corner. "Give up now kid," one said.

Mato responded with a barrage of laser fire, frying the pirate's head right off. This caused the remaining pirate to retreat, either to gather more forces or try his luck facing CJ after the battle. Wielding dual pistols, Mato turned into a force to be reckoned with. Taryn led from between the two men, looking at a data pad and giving directions. A turn here, a turn there. Sometimes straight and sometimes they had to find a hidden passage.

Jay stared down a new hallway filled with doors and numbered rooms. "This doesn't look like a way out."

"Trust me," said Taryn.

The sounds of laser fire quieted for a bit as they walked down the surprising squeaky hallway. The room doors were reinforced metal. The floor was made out of a loose material that made noise with every step. Jay stomped past locked doors that had a big red light above them, presumably signaling which ones were open and which ones which were closed. None of them had the green open light, so Jay proceeded without any caution.

"We should be quiet. I don't want to wake any of the guests," said Taryn.

"There are guests in there? What are they doing?" asked Mato as he knocked on one of the doors.

"Quit that. I'll have one of your parents explain it if we ever make it out of here," said Taryn.

"I think we are way past not waking the locals," said Jay. He pointed his rifle straight up and fired two quick shots.

Mato smiled, *I like this guy.* There were at least twenty rooms left in the hall they were trying to walk past when a light turned green just behind Jay, the door below it split in half, and a pirate tried to grab Jay's rifle. He had to use it as a bat to beat the pirates off of him. He blooded their bodies and hit them with so much blunt force that their skins ripped. More lights turned green as doors opened. Taryn was assaulted by a pirate with a shock baton and a collar he tried to get around her neck. Taryn moved her hand up against his momentum, causing him to stumble backward. The collar snapped back and forth like it was alive. Blades clicked in and out along its interior, creating an unusual circular weapon that Taryn tried to avoid. She ducked low and took out the pirate's feet, and he fell; this was precisely what she wanted to happen. She grabbed his weapon and shocked the pirate, causing him to drop the snapping collar which fell, making a loud clanking on the squeaky floor.

Mato spread his arms out wide, using his pistols to cover both doors parallel to him in the hallway. He fired over and around his companions as they battled pirates that tried to capture the group as they passed by. The pirates would open a door then close it immediately, sometimes coming out of the same room, sometimes moving in the background and coming out of a different room creating confusion. Mato smiled, this was something that he finally felt confident in. He traded the pistols with Taryn for her baton, finding another on the floor from a downed pirate. Mato swung the sticks, hitting pirates and stopping them in place. They would shrivel up, shake, and convulse as he shocked the life out of them. Taryn, now forced to use a pistol, fired at any pirate that crossed her path. She adjusted the laser pulse on the gun quickly, this allowed her to fire indirectly at the pirates. The laser would bounce off the walls of the station and hit the pirates from behind, from above, and any angle she thought they would not expect.

The doors continued to open while Mato shocked pirates, sometimes leaving them in the doorways as it would shut again, causing the pirate in the way to be cut in half. Blood began to spill all over the floor. Not only did it squeak, it now splashed when they walked. Taryn banked and reflected laser shots, hitting pirates who hid behind their compatriots and those that tried to shoot back and fire shots from a distance.

Jay led with his laser, marching down the hallway putting multiple well-aimed shots at anyone that sprang out from either side of him. They slowly made their way down the hall as the doors stopped opening. After what seemed like an hour of fighting only a couple of minutes had actually passed, they reached the end.

"Open this door," Taryn ordered. The red lights still glowing washed out the color of the blood that flowed beneath it. The hallway was now littered with pirate bodies. Their dead, unwashed flesh smelled even more foul than normal. Without missing a beat, Jay picked up a severed pirate head and smashed it into the door. Its sensor triggered, and the three interlopers rushed in. Taryn looked at schematics at on her datapad.

"What are you looking at?" said Mato.

"I'm looking at a secret passage," Taryn replied.

"Where? I don't see it. How can you tell?" asked Mato.

Taryn put down the pad and lifted a rug from the overly soft looking room. Its soft fabrics and bright colors contrasted against the cold iron and steel look of the walls. Taryn pulled the rug back and had Jay moved a nearby bed. There they found a hatch hidden in the floor. They opened it and were about to climb in.

Jay surveyed the room. Surprised, he found an undamaged utility belt on one of the pirates. A large scoring hole was apparent on the pirate's back, an obvious sign Taryn had shot him while he was looking the other way.

"Grenades. These will be useful," said Jay.

"Can I have one?" asked Mato.

"I think we should leave these to the experienced team members."

Taryn nodded in agreement.

Mato folded his arms and shook his head. "I'm already the best fighter," he suggested.

"Whatever you say, kid," said Jay as he jumped down into the hole after Taryn. Mato took an interest in following last and shadowing Jay for the time being.

Taryn led them through maintenance shafts, small narrow corridors that Jay could barely fit through. Then they went down into a room on the next floor. They interrupted a man sitting in the corner watching a couple of ladies. The ladies rushed to cover up, and the man ran away into the bathroom screaming for security.

"This is not what I paid for!" he yelled as they uncovered another secret passage in the middle of the floor that led to another lower level.

Mato turned his head and stared at the ladies. They weren't dressed properly, and they were beautiful to him.

"First set of tits you have seen that wasn't cloned huh?" Jay asked.

"NO," responded Mato.

"Sure, don't stare too long. You don't want ladies like those noticing you. You aren't ready for what they have to give," said Jay as he heard the next hatch open.

They climbed down and entered another room. This time it was inhabited by only one woman. She screamed at the sudden intrusion.

"I don't know what you think is about to happen, but it's not going down like this!" She yelled as she swung a chair at them.

"Calm down we will be out of your way in no time," said Jay.

Taryn unlocked the door from her datapad.

"Why didn't you do that earlier?" asked Jay.

"It's easier trying to get out than in. At least from most rooms," said Taryn.

The room's occupant left swinging her chair in the air, and she spat at Mato. Jay grabbed his arm and rushed him out the door, into the hall to follow Taryn.

"Are Nattie ladies always this hostile?" asked Mato to Jay as they ran down another hallway.

"Every single one kid. Ain't that right, Taryn?" said Jay.

"He's right."

"The airlock we are looking for is down by the main ballroom. It should be just down this hall and past those doors. The ones right there." She opened them from her datapad.

"You mean with Midnight's personal guards in the way," said Jay.

The white face paint and black armored outfitted guards stood silent and eerily waiting for the group to approach. They didn't raise their hands or move their bodies in an act of aggression; they stood silently and just turned their masked heads in their direction. Mato moved to rush forward with shock batons.

"No wait," said Jay.

"Stop!" screamed Taryn as the clone ran forward, his head low and his batons at his sides. Mato parried and swung widely. He jumped on the walls to get more leverage and then struck down hard. The masked guards blocked him, using little effort. They used the backs of their arms and legs as shields from Mato's attacks. Mato took the baton and struck out, placing both of the offensive ends of the batons directly on the guards that were in front of him, and to his shock, nothing happened. They didn't show any signs of pain or any motion at all. They stood, silent and unmoving until a backhand struck the side of Mato's face, sending him spinning back towards Jay and Taryn. He fell on his back and was unconscious. Taryn fired while Jay re-cocked his rifle.

"Still got that trick from earlier?" She asked.

"No need I got grenades," said Jay.

Taryn's eyes grew wide as she turned, and ran in the opposite direction.

Jay stepped in front of Mato's prone form, popped the cap off an inversion grenade and threw it forward. A blue light appeared out of the small cylinder device, followed by a glowing field, then the sucking sound of compression. The guards had enough time to push themselves back and away from the blast. Jay threw three more in quick succession. A clear black reflective sheet came out of the armor of each guard and surrounded the grenades. It effectively neutralized their inversion fields, causing them to putter out instead of making their loud sucking sounds. Jay had one more grenade but decided not to use it because it wasn't successful so far. The guards, in unison, put their black-gloved hands out and waved their fingers backward inviting Jay in. Jay threw the rifle behind him.

"You know what to do," he said to Taryn who was down the hall watching and awaiting the outcome of the present encounter.

Jay moved in and punched broadly. The two guards moved and avoided his advances. He swept and rolled his leg trying to surprise the guards with a roundhouse kick that didn't connect. They punched Jay, their gloved hands transferring force to his exposed skin. The left guard connected with Jay's midsection with a pop. Jay felt pain shear through his body. *Fuck, a broken rib.* The other guard swept his legs causing Jay to fall on his back. He looked up and saw the ceiling before a boot was placed on his face. The other guard fell down to pin Jay to the ground while the other kicked and punched him. He felt the exhaustion and fatigue of being hit until he couldn't move. Every muscle ached, and the pain from having someone sit on his cracked rib was unbearable. Using all the power he could muster, it felt like every muscle in his body responded, he grabbed the guard's foot and dragged him down as he rolled himself up. Suddenly Jay was on top. He pummeled the guards with furious kicks and punches until he could not give any more. The white outlines of their faces looked up at him as he seemed to tire them out. That's when the masks flashed at him in a blinding light with holovids of terrifying images of his teammates dying, along with edited vids of his current group dying in horrible ways. This made Jay doubt reality for just a second. He looked back at Taryn who was standing away from the action, relatively safe and unharmed, while Mato still laid on the floor forgotten in the skirmish. That momentary distraction was all the guards needed to get back on the offensive. They attacked, hitting Jay in the midsection again. Another pop sound, another rib was broken. Blood started to spill from his mouth. In the background, he saw that Taryn had a small glowing orb next to her.

"Taryn, now's the time!" he yelled. She ejected the battery pack from the rifle, and the orb flew through the hall. The guards were too distracted to notice the orb as it drifted and collided with them. It exploded on their backs, killing the first guard instantly. The second was caught in a trap of black goo as the anti-grenade device on the first guard's front went into overdrive, sending sheet after sheet of countermeasure onto the other guard, wrapping the guard's arms and shoulders, gluing him to the wall.

"That was easy," said Taryn. She ran her fingers through her hair in an attempt to lighten the stress the fight had put on her emotions.

Jay was on the ground. "I'm beat up pretty bad. I'm too old for this shit."

Taryn rushed to him. "Is there anything I can do?" she asked.

Jay lifted his arm up. Taryn grabbed it and let her body fall backward to help her pull the huge man to his feet. This provided Jay with enough leverage to pick himself up from the floor.

"We can't stop now," said Jay. He gave a hearty kick to Mato's side, waking him. "Come we have to get out of here."

"That is going to be easier said than done," said Taryn from the ballroom.

The ballroom had a glass floor that dipped down in a hexagon shape one to two steps down from a beveled glass pane. This allowed one to look down to the level below. Velvet tapestries lined the walls in plain bold colors. The room had a giant chandelier that soaked the room in a warm glow. There was only a little bit of black trim that lined the walls and edges of the floor. The glass floor had a slight smoked tint to it, giving an extra sense of extravagance to an already overwhelming sight.

Taryn looked down below to the view of CJ holding a revolving blaster to Eyota's head.

CJ stared up at the three of them through the floor. She had a group of pirates and four of Midnight's black guards standing around her in a circle. They stood guard, and everyone's eyes were on Jay. Taryn walked to the back edge of the center hexagon. She stood where the steps met the lower level of the floor.

"Give up, or this rich and connected citizen of the GPL gets it," said CJ through the speaker system of the ballroom.

"I don't care about him. He is just a wealthy man like any other. He has no significance in the scientific community," said Taryn.

CJ's eye squinted, and her finger seemed to tighten around the trigger making her threat more immediate.

"You don't have to do this. I can make you all rich. No need to fight ever again," said Eyota.

"Shut up. You don't need to be alive for us pirates to make money off you," said CJ.

Eyota swallowed heavily.

"CJ. You wait there. Once I find a way down there, I'm going to rip you into pieces."

"Eahhyaa!"

"What was that?" asked Taryn.

"Oh, that? A little surprise I left for you. My man is out of the icebox," said CJ.

Jax roared as he swung violently into view. He had come from the other direction, hidden behind the tapestries that lined the ballroom. Jax turned at Taryn who ducked and ran away from him, moving around on the floor trying to avoid Jax at all cost. Jay punched and kicked his old friend desperately. Jax stood there like a brick wall and took every hit. Jay was connecting, but his hits had no effect. Jax roared again, spreading his arms out as he wrapped Jay in a bear hug, head-butting him, sending an explosion on blood from Jay's face. Jay screamed out in pain from his broken ribs. Jax tossed him to the side and set his sights on Mato.

Mato almost cowered as he backed away from the approaching monster of rage. Holding a grenade in his hand Mato made eye contact with Eyota.

Galactic Mandate: The Scream

"Don't do it," Eyota screamed as CJ took the back of her gun and hit him in the head, knocking him to the floor.

Mato looked around at Taryn who was now across the floor pulling herself backward and away, trying to make it before the eventual outcome of coming fight. Jax came at Mato, swinging his arms, trying to connect with all the force his rage-fueled brain could muster. Knocking his knuckles on the glass floor and cutting them open, Jax kept swinging. Mato duck and dodged, keeping distance. His young body and lean frame made him two to three times as fast as the rage-filled ex-soldier who moved in slow, powerful thrusts. Popping the lid on the grenade, Mato dropped it on the floor. The pirates, guards, and CJ below didn't have time to react as the floor shattered and came crashing down. Everyone on the upper level fell to the level below. Sharp blades of glass rained on them all.

Sharp sounds of glass as it continued to fall onto soft skin filled the space station's main entry room. Blood drenched the floors, and cries and screams echoed off the walls. Soon, groaning was the background noise to the sounds Mato made dragging the members of his group clear of the damaged area, trying to avoid the broken glass. Shards rubbed against Jay's bare skin as Mato dragged him into the pirate ship. Mato grabbed Jay first because of his wounds. Taryn was next. She was severely cut as well. He pulled her into the vessel and plopped her next to what looked to be the most critical computer position on the bridge. Everyone in the room who was still alive wheezed as they bled. Mato found Eyota in a corner. He looked a lot better than the rest of the people in the room.

"Looks like you have saved me again," he said.

"I'm not sure if I have," said Mato. He reached and grabbed Eyota, but she resisted and pushed away.

"Leave me here. I have to look after the clones." Eyota pulled himself to his feet and moved towards a maintenance portal.

Mato crumpled his lips and looked around as he walked away. "We need you now more than ever," Mato said, closing the airlock behind him.

The doors to the station entrance were blasted open. A squadron of Midnight's Blackguard entered and secured the room. She saw Jax's dead body piled on top of some pirates who were still alive. They groaned and scratched each other because of Jax's poison blood. The rage infected them, and they tried to lash out with their broken bodies.

"Do you want us to end them?" the guards asked.

"No. Don't waste the effort. No one in this room has much time left."

The guards started picking over the bodies for survivors while Midnight towered over CJ.

"I'm disappointed in you," said Midnight. CJ whimpered as the glass puncturing her drained her of blood. "Doesn't look like you will be winning any beauty contest at any time soon," Midnight continued. She turned datapad into a mirror and showed it to CJ who screamed at the sight before her.

"Turn on the station defenses. I want that carrier destroyed," Midnight ordered.

"We can't it's too close," the guards replied.

"Then get in the other ships and blast it!"

***

Mato slapped Taryn. "Wake up. I need you to run the ship."

The woman eyes shifted, and she seemed to come slowly back to reality.

"Where am I?" she asked.

"I dragged you on the pirate ship."

"I hurt all over," she replied.

"We don't have time for that. Look," Mato pointed at a threat awareness warning on the monitors. It showed a zoomed in view of the other two ships raising and priming their weapons.

"I need a doctor," Taryn replied.

"Yes, you do. Please send us to one," begged Mato as he slapped her again.

"Alright, alright. Stop slapping me and get to work," said Taryn.

"I don't understand how any of this works," said Mato.

"Then move out of the way."

"Hey you're not the captain," said two workers as they rounded the corner and moved onto the bridge.

Mato charged them and grabbed the shirt of the first worker, ripping it as he pulled the worker forward. "I've been captured, beaten, and all of your shit pirates that have tried to kill me are lying in a pile of their own blood. And the only adults who have been nice to me are messed up! Help my friends, or I'm going to space you," Mato yelled as he pushed off the workers shoving them backward.

"We can put your friend in stasis. The big one there. We can keep him alive," one stuttered.

"At least long enough to get where you are going," said the other.

"You better," Mato demanded.

Taryn found the station she sitting at was able to open to all systems of the ship and turned them on. She was able to get weapons, navigation, and the zero drive, but not the sub-light navigation. She looked up and stared at the space station. *It's the docking clamps.*

"The station. I wondered why it hasn't blown us to bits. We must be too close for their targeting systems."

The ship rocked, and the lights flickered. The other docked carriers had been released and were starting an assault attempt to destroy the ship while it was still anchored. The lights flickered again as the ship began to take damage.

"Can't we shoot back?" Mato asked.

"Calm down. I don't tell you how to throw rocks, don't tell me how to operate," said Taryn

"Throw rocks? I saved us."

"Shut up. I need to think."

Luckily, they were on the ship with the special artifact. *I wonder what it can do. Can I use it to bend the laws of zero space and get out of here without sublight?* She tried to access the drive, and it didn't respond. *Shit, the pirates messed with it again. Why would they do that?* She asked herself. *I'll have to experiment with the artifacts some other time. Artifacts. Wait a minute.* She pulled the artifact she recovered from the Clones and got up and ran to another station on the bridge. She wondered where all the energy came from and how she could now move like she was not in pain from all the cuts that had been inflicted from the glass floor's collapse. Making a makeshift plugin from spare parts, she hooked up the artifact to the pirate vessel. Modulating the shields, the flickering the lights stopped, and the ship stopped taking damage. The ship started to absorb the energy from each shot from the other vessels.

This didn't stop them from trying to cause damage. The Black Guard fired and tried different frequencies. The attempts no longer had any effect on the carrier.

"Ignorant fools," Taryn muttered to herself.

She held her hand over the weapon controls. The lights indication for the intensity and power loads were all flashing and indicating that the ship was heading for overload. This had pushed its components to the max. The heat was starting to build up, which was unusual before the weapons were fired.

"Time to show them why you don't mess with a scientist," Taryn thought.

She pressed the "Fire Weapons" button as her fingers started to move in rapid speed as she typed in trajectories and listed her targets. She moved the many cannons around and had them pointed in three directions, one at each of the other two carriers and the last at the space station.

The laser cannons fired with dramatic intensity, shredding the other ships, and ripping off the docked ends of the vessel. The station was armored and could take a hit. It was made to defend against a fleet of ships, and Midnight was lucky she had chosen it because it took immense damage.

The armor plating had shredded, and gun mountings fell off the station and floated in space with other debris. The station was severely damaged, but its internal structure was not. Its exterior armor, weapons, and docking bays could no longer be used. Taryn's modified weapons did the damage equivalent of an entire fleet. She looked out the main viewport and admired her work. Taryn was saddened that she was happy about destruction but proud that the devastation she caused was beyond the scope of anyone else with the resources used.

The ship was free of the docking clamps and steadily cruising away from the space station.

"Are they all dead?" asked Mato.

"No, they are fine. Defenseless but they are fine. Hopefully, they don't have any rivals," Taryn replied.

"They don't look fine," said Mato

"It's time for zero space. Get ready ok?"

Chapter 12

"Taryn, wake up," said Mato as he shook her.

"Where am I?" she asked.

"A place I hate so far," said Mato.

Taryn noticed he was wearing something very familiar to her. A translation helmet. It was impossible to miss as it covered the face from the ears up. What he spoke was converted to signed language. That was displayed in front of his face while he talked. The language was foreign even though it was supposed to be her native tongue.

This is not the language of the science I know, she told herself. The young man continued to shake her until she pushed him off and removed her face mask. She unhooked herself form wires and tubes that were attached to her body. She could see that she had been placed on a long body slab, and Jay lay on the next one over. There was a third which must have been a space for Mato as well.

"How long has it been?" she asked worriedly. That she was put into cryo without her knowledge bothered her.

"Only a week," Mato replied. "I need help waking Jay. He won't wake up. I tried him first but switched after I gave up on it," said Mato.

"We can wake him, but I need a minute," Taryn said as she got up. She needed Mato's help as her legs were weak. She surveyed the room and looked around, leaning against a wall for support.

"Here," said Mato. He handed her a datapad that showed Jay's vitals. She turned to let her back lean against the wall. This gave her more room to manipulate the information on the datapad. She tried the essential functions for waking Jay. Then she went into more advanced systems. The system showed that he was awake, but she clearly saw that that wasn't the truth. He lay there breathing but didn't move his body; it was no longer repairing itself. Thinking it was a technical glitch with the computer systems, she moved into the program, checking its code and trying to diagnose the problem.

"What's wrong with him?" asked Mato.

"Not sure, something isn't correct. This doesn't make sense. They aren't known for faulty systems."

"I did the same thing to wake you and him. He's just still asleep."

"Yes, I can see that. The problem isn't technical; we need a doctor," said Taryn.

"Great. We haven't been welcomed with open arms. They are not going to give us a doctor. They barely give me enough food. It was better on the reservation than here," said Mato

Their conversation was interrupted by the entrance of four armed guards with one man in the middle. He gestured for Mato to pick up the translation helmet.

"I'm sure he'll wake up soon enough," signed the man in the middle. "I'm Ismag. I'm here to take you to The Magistrate, our leader."

"Great, him again. The man won't shut up. He talks so much. Well, signs so much I guess," said Mato.

"I would be careful whom you insult, boy. You are only here because of his hospitality and generosity. That could change at any moment," signed Ismag.

Taryn placed the datapad down and moved forward. She looked at the guards and their strange weapons that were much more substantial and squarer barreled than she was used to seeing and pondering how they worked. Mato followed suit, and they walked behind Ismag as he led them down halls. They had small egress windows that looked out over a rocky, barren planet nothing but dark rocks that appeared almost black in color.

"Why do you live here?" Mato asked, amazed that there was almost no life outside.

"Because we can." Ismag signed. They continued their walking until they reached the entrance to a large circle conference room. A large wooden slab floated in the middle of the room. Several people were sitting and watched as their leader, The Magistrate, stood and welcomed the two in.

The leader didn't waste any time. His hands started moving at furious speed. Taryn tried to stop them by saying, "I don't understand. I don't speak this language."

Everyone in the room looked at her mouth and seemed to be confused. She repeated herself, and a guard approached her with a translation helmet. She placed it on her head, and now she could hear each word that was signed to her instantly as it was translated by the helmet and then spoken in her ear.

The Magistrate started again.

"We are glad to have you here. The ship you have brought us had some very unique properties. It is the key to what we have been searching for," he signed.

Taryn's stomach turned. She had an awful feeling, and she spoke out immediately.

"You can't steal my research. That ship is the property of the GPL!" she interrupted. The helmet translated her words into hand signals.

"I had hoped you would be of a different mind," signed The Magistrate. The others shook their heads in unison.

"Perhaps if I give you a tour of what we are working on you will change your mind and maybe even your allegiance. This is cutting-edge science. I know you will want to be a part of it instead of just a stepping stone."

Taryn was shocked. No one had spoken, whether spoken or signed, to her that way in a long time not since her first day at the academy. Everyone thought she was just a young push over prodigy, that she was moved up incorrectly, that she couldn't be as smart as everyone said she was.

"If you have science to show I'll gladly accept, but I will not tolerate the theft of my research," said Taryn.

"You do not understand. Everything you do from now on will go to help us. We are The Scream, and we do not take no for an answer. You just need some time to understand. Take her away. We will resume this tomorrow," signed The Magistrate.

The guards closed in and grabbed her shoulders. They did the same to Mato. They were escorted back to the room she had originally awakened. The door slammed behind them after they had thrown both Taryn and Mato.

"Do you hear that?" asked Mato as he took off his helmet. "Everything around here seems to emit a whining."

"Yes, The Scream doesn't care about noise, so their electronics tend to emit high pitch whining that others don't," Taryn replied.

"It's been annoying me since I got here. I can't stand it," said Mato.

"Just ignore it. We won't be here forever."

"How do you know that?" Mato replied.

"I just do." Taryn took off her helmet then immediately found some tools lying around the room. She popped the helmet open and connected it to the data pad. Looking through its electronics and its software she was able to find a small device that was designed to spy on them. That was how they knew so soon that she'd woken up. She disabled it and then grabbed Mato's helmet.

"Hey what are you doing?" he asked.

"I'm making it so we can have a private conversation," she replied.

"Won't they just put their ear to the door?" he asked.

"Since they are all deaf it won't help them anyway."

"Oh!" Mato handed over the helmet. She opened it up and disabled it in half the time it took her with the first one.

"We do need to think of a way to get out of this mess. I'm not letting The Scream take credit for my research," said Taryn.

"The Magistrate seems set on you working for him,"

"That won't happen. I'm loyal to The Galactic Planetary League. Betraying the galaxy is something I won't do, it is wrong."

"Maybe you should just lie. On the reservation, our leaders did it all the time. It was bad. They would say one thing then do another. You Natties probably wouldn't know what that is like having the governments of the galaxy come to tell you what they will do then they just won't do it. Or sometimes they would even come back and do the opposite. It's hard being a clone without the CDF around," said Mato.

"I find your limited view of the world amusing, but you just might have a point," said Taryn.

"We better get to sleep. The Scraem?"

"The Scream." Taryn corrected.

"Well, they like to get up early and drag us around the base."

"All right," she replied. Then she crawled on to the slab that she'd woken up on. She moved the excess wires and laid her head on the folded pillow of her arm. Then she fell asleep.

In the morning, she was awoken by The Magistrate himself. His personal guards stood next to Ismag who followed closely behind. Taryn reached down and put on her helmet as The Magistrate was already signing away. She watched his hands move. *It would be easier to just learn their language, but that is beneath me.*

"I have something to show you," signed The Magistrate. He motioned for her to follow along.

"We need a doctor. We need to wake up our friend."

"Is he a scientist?"

"No, he's a soldier," she replied.

"Then let the boy handle it. The soldier won't be of much use where we are going," signed The Magistrate.

He led her down a lone hall and corridor into another large circular facility. It sprouted up from the landscape. The hallway worked as a small highway for people to walk and take small transports down. It looked like it had been cleared for The Magistrate's walk with Taryn.

"Where are we going?" Taryn asked, bored with the walk and the rocky, barren scenery that she studied through the windows.

"To a lab. It's so important I don't store it on world. The other leaders of The Scream don't trust anyone. Security for what we are working and who is helping is the utmost importance," The Magistrate signed.

She followed with Ismag watching her every move as they reached the middle of the tower. It led to the space elevator. This took them up to the ship floating above the planet. The pride of The Scream fleet. *The Kiladon.* It was rumored that the design for *The Desolution* was based on it. The massive ship was the largest in the galaxy. It was ten times the size of one of the pirate cruisers and twice the size of *The Desolution.*

From the elevator, she could see the planet which they left. The cities glowed unusually bright the population centers were as one single large dot of light. Spaced out all over the planet, they glowed as red dots against a dark world.

Galactic Mandate: The Scream

"Our homeworld, Si La, is one of the most beautiful don't you think?" The Magistrate asked.

Absolutely not. She thought, but her more calm and diplomatic side had to come out to respond to the current question. Even she wasn't that socially unaware as to know that it would not be considered polite to respond in such a way.

"Yes, I agree," was the only thing she was able to mutter. The translation helmet seemed to glow dimly as she said this, as if it was aware that she was unsure about what she just said.

"We are almost there," said The Magistrate. He rocked back and forth in place. He seemed to be impatient and almost giddy about what he was about to show her.

Gradually their skin turned pale white as they entered space, as did hers.

"Ah, you are one of us," The Magistrate signed.

"Only by birth," Taryn replied. His eyes were fixated at her helmet. Taryn grew uneasy with the stare but knew it was necessary.

"You should really learn our language. The language of your people. If you choose to join us voluntarily, we will welcome you with open arms." This was more literal than she expected as his arms spread far apart in a simulated hug.

"My mother had to smuggle me out. You consider me a genetic defect. People like me aren't allowed to stay in the silent empire. Show me what you are about to show me and be done with it," said Taryn.

"So be it," signed The Magistrate.

They arrived on the massive ship and were escorted by a delighted ship captain. Taryn looked away from him so that her translation device wouldn't speak up the small talk and meaningless pleasantries that the captain bestowed upon The Magistrate.

Taryn grew impatient, and her helmet started to pick up the tail end of the captain's and The Magistrate's conversation.

"Do you want to take the shortcut or do you want the full tour."

Please take the shortcut. I can't stand being idle for this long. Taryn thought. Being too close and at the wrong position, Taryn couldn't catch what The Magistrate was signing as a response. *Hopefully, he means the shortcut.*

Chapter 13

Fractal punched then butted his head forward, missing his opponent entirely.

"Go for the legs," the voice told him as he swept. Variant was waiting, his moves calculated and prepared.

"Go right."

"No, go left."

"Punch"

"Kick," said the voices as they disagreed and argued. Fractal disagreed but couldn't decipher which voice was his and which was the others. He and his brother Variant were unique in this. They both heard them. They came nice and organized to Variant. He would talk to them, deciding the best course of action. Fractal could only argue but somethings he could tell if it was him arguing or another. He got lost in the noise whereas Variant just heard clarity.

Did he listen to the voice that told him to cheat? Fractal couldn't say, he just knew that his knuckles felt heavy. He didn't want to harm his brother, but he wasn't the only opinion in control of his body. Fractal swung and kicked, letting his guard down so that he could attack even more. Sometimes he would allow the others to take control and let the personalities move forward to do what they wanted as he sat in the background watching. Fractal was dominant. He was the "new" as the other personalities called him. The baby, they would tease. They were great men, to be admired. Sometimes he would look up their information, see what they were doing in the world to settle the voices. This would give him peace for a while.

His attacks had little effect, but they made the crowd roar. The sound was pumped in from the speakers. Schools of fish would dissipate when his attacks would land on the walls sending a massive shockwave of a pinging sound through the hexagon enclosure.

Galactic Mandate: The Scream

Fractal looked to Dark Cleo as she leaned against the wall, her presence intruding on their match. She looked off into the distance of the deep ocean and watched what little production was still ongoing of the secret fleet. Her arms were crossed, and her uniform was pristine. Even with the rugged wear, she would give her clothes, she never missed a press, never had a fold in the suit missing. She said she did this for her father, but Fractal knew better. Her father spoke to him in his head. He said she was always this way. Or was that her father? Fractal could never be sure. The voices, they shared their identities, but unlike his brother, he would forget and have to be reminded by them.

Variant countered. Fractal tried to rely on his training and do the combination he had been taught in the military training school. Variant was there for every blow with the perfect counter. The voices took over, and he cackled with a strange sureness that created an odd evil sound. The bets around them swarmed in as waves of cash were being wagered. Then blackness.

Fractal came to with Dark Cleo holding him down. He had her on his left arm bending it almost in half and Variant blooded and beaten on the other. They pulled as he screamed out in pain. Blood was running down his face. His vision was blurry, and Variant laughed in his usual smugness.

I must have fallen into one of his traps again.

Variant was always three steps ahead. The voices allowed him to play chess with each personality while everyone else was playing with sticks. Fractal wished they tormented Variant like they tormented him, but wishing was not going to do anything. Guards rushed in and stopped the fight; it was over. The bookies registered it as a win for Variant, and he gave a laugh. One that Fractal knew all too well as it had a slight change in pitch with each person that took over it. Something that everyone else seemed to have missed.

"Rematch!" Fractal screamed. He repeated himself over and over. The crowd loved it.

Dark Cleo leaned and tried to calm the enraged teenager. "It's just a match."

"No, it's my pride. It's all of our pride," Fractal replied.

"Settle down. That is an order."

"You don't order me, mother. I am all of you," replied Fractal.

"Another week in the white room for you." Variant teased.

"Take him away. Don't bring him back until he's back to normal," said, Dark Cleo.

"Mother no!" shouted Fractal.

Chapter 14

Taryn was very glad to see that The Magistrate had chosen the shortcut. Finally, I can get back to work. Wait what am I thinking? I shouldn't work for these, these, Eugenicists. They moved to a shuttle.

"What is this?"

"The ship is so large, this shuttle will fly her to the new lab. It was preparing for our last guest. I think you will like him once you meet." Taryn shrugged as the shuttle rose above its docking bay. It floated above about fourteen decks of the ship before it settled on its own docking ledge in the controlled environment.

"Why not just use an elevator?" Taryn asked.

"Like the captain said this is a shortcut. It's not permanent," said The Magistrate.

"Open the door" The Magistrate commanded. Taryn followed the orders and moved outside of the shuttle then moved to two large doors guarded by Machine Men. They were frame muscles and stood in a cold statue-like pose. Their red eyes followed Taryn as she approached the laboratory doors. The cold metal steel color of their wide frame bodies made Taryn shiver and stop her progress.

"It's ok to go on," said The Magistrate as the Machine Men moved their heads back into a forward position, their eyes no longer following the procession of officials as they came to observe the laboratory. The guards looked at each other then continued their cold stares into nothingness. These guards wore decorative cloth in between the wireframes of their arms and a decorative loincloth that dragged on the floor.

Inside the laboratory, a metal head was floating a yellowish liquid attached to the back wall. Giant monitors displayed formula she assumed the head was working on. Her eyes were immediately drawn to them. She recognized these equations.

"You are working on the artifacts!" she announced.

"Why yes. We are. We resurrected the remains of Dr. Ulises Tom and found the key to our future. Ever since we lost the genetic war and the invasion of The Acolytes failed to take hold, we have been looking for something to finally break the logjam of our fight with the rest of the galaxy," The Magistrate explained.

"You think linking the artifacts to your ships will enable you to wield ships with enough power to overwhelm the combined forces of the empire of the GPL. Even with a dozen of these artifacts that just won't happen," said Taryn.

"With yours and the doctors help we won't need to," said The Magistrate.

"I don't understand."

"She is all yours doctor," The Magistrate said to the floating head of Ulises Tom. The monitors changed to project a holographic presentation of Ulises Tom's head that always looked forwards while its dark red eyes looked at Taryn.

"I've been following your research in the GPL. We are both working on the artifacts, but I much grander plans for them. Turn around I'll show you."

Reluctant to turn her back on the large holograms she turned and looked. She saw the color-coded holder for the artifacts. How could I miss that?

"The deep red artifact is the one that the pirates had attached to its zero drive. I recognized some of the code in its maintenance program. Have you been moonlighting as a pirate? Taryn?" asked the doctor.

"Just some repairs for the barbarians while I studied their artifact. The pirates had no idea what they had in their possession," said Taryn

"Just like you," said the doctor.

Taryn turned back around and pointed her finger at the hologram.

"Listen here! I am the lead scientist of the GPL. Not some backwater con artist who feels superior just because he converted himself to a Machine Man," she lectured.

"Disappointing. I expected so much more from you," said the doctor. "Now please don't interrupt. I have more to present."

Galactic Mandate: The Scream

The podium split and two more artifacts rose from the middle of the structure. They had green and bright orange labels. Taryn's eyes went wide as she saw her goal being presented to her. Another artifact! This was the one that The Scream controlled. She wondered how they were using it. She crossed her arms and then moved to the side almost looking away from the podium in protest.

"The forest green artifact is the other we commandeered from that what I am sure was a filthy pirate ship. It's ability to absorb all types of energies is truly impressive. Enough of what I have gotten The Scream to take from you. Let me show you what they have to offer."

The orange artifact moved up and was lifted up by a repulsing field. Taryn reached out for it but was met by a slight shock. It was enough to make reflexes react and pull her hand back.

"This one is the source of The Scream's power. It is what makes all the sonic weapons so dangerous."

"How is that possible? I've seen what their weapons can do. The GPL has never been able to replicate the power of their sonic guns."

"That is because they have you for their scientist. The Scream have me."

"You mean they have that artifact. I don't see your contribution was anything more than creating generic copies and placing them in the guns. Something a low-level industrialist could easily do with anything more than a week and those people can barely put on their boots without help," Taryn retorted.

"How dare you insult my research! I bet you don't even know what the true purpose of what this technology is for."

"Are you telling me you don't think I know what my own cutting-edge research is all about? These artifacts are going to be key to opening a portal that will lead us to discover new galaxies. The increased space will reduce the aggression of the GPL Empire and provide an era for peace," Taryn again lectured the floating head.

"I have never been able to perceive it, but what you just said, I can only assume is humor. Thank you for that. I finally understand what funny is. How naive you are for being so scientifically talented is amazing. You know nothing of human nature, and you know nothing of the artifacts. They are not tools of destructions, and they are not keys to a new world, they are not the path to peace. They are beacons," said Ulises Tom.

The holograms ceased and were replaced by video footage of a remote station that Taryn was not familiar with, along with text in an ancient language that looked arcane and evil.

"What is this?" Taryn demanded.

"I found instructions in my expeditions."

The video changed to displayed a temple that was on Emortono. This was one that she knew, but again it gave the same arcane feel.

"I know this temple, but I've never seen this part of it."

"Of course not. This is what you find when you look deeper. When you are above the cutting edge and are on another level," the head bragged. Its eyes glowed while it was in its floating enclosure.

"Fascinating," the words slipped from Taryn's mouth.

"Indeed. Do you see? You have so much to learn, but your assistance is necessary. Even though your research is inferior, it is still essential. You are going to be the most useful assistant that I could find. The Scream, they are useless when it comes to this endeavor. That is why they are supporting my research. I support them, and they support me," said Ulises Tom

"How can The Magistrate agree to this?" Taryn asked.

"He knows the beacon will lead to the destruction of his enemies. Like the rest of humanity, he can't think about more than the short-term satisfaction of revenge. He can barely focus on what is not in front of him. He can't see the scale of desolation that these beacons will bring. It makes me wish I had a body again just so I could feel the chills run down my spine. Join me as I destroy the entire galaxy," said Ulises Tom.

Taryn tried to swallow her pride. The advice of the young clone rang in her ears. Just make him happy, she thought. I need time to stop this evil. "What do you need me to do?"

***

Taryn woke up again. The guards said it was time for her to make the commute to The Kiladon. Taryn witnessed the difference no longer being escorted by a dignitary made. She could no longer move down entirely hallways alone. Now she moved in crowded space, and none of the locals bothered to stop and read her helmet whenever she tried to communicate. They seemed to be disinterested in what she had to say. Having an experience like this was new for her. Not since she was a tiny child had people ignored her presence. She wondered if this was what it was like to live like a normal person in the galaxy, with no more significant purpose but to be a cog in the machine that she designed.

Eventually, she walked off the shuttle past her Machine Men guards. She thought of her commute. Being a commoner sure was time-consuming. She wondered how anyone could waste so much of their time moving from place to place and not having a project to work on even if it was for pure evil. She shook her head, switched her skin color and put on a smile. The floating head seemed to underestimate her when there was a smile on her face. It gave her an advantage that could easily distract its evil peering eyes.

"We are creating a controller that can channel the power of multiple artifacts to open up the beacon. The GPL has the last artifact, but we won't need that once we create a replacement. We will have the power of gods. Even The Acolytes will bow to the power of Ulises Tom. Do you understand Taryn?" She gave a big toothy smiled and went to work.

Chapter 15

Mato slipped out of his room. The guards tried to chase him, but they could not keep up with his youthful speed and the agility that Mato gained from growing up on the reservation. He moved up and around objects. They couldn't keep up. He walked up and left into a facility that was open and circular. Mato was amazed to find children in the room. He looked around. He tried to find their parents, but all he saw were fetuses. Rectangular towers went from the floor to the ceiling with babies being incubated in the middle. They were floating in a small sea of different color liquids while in a tiny transparent bundle. Little children ran around and played with floating balls that bounced softly off the wall and around the facility.

"Who are you? Are you clones?" Mato asked. They held their mouths and laughed without noise as some children grabbed each other, engaged in a game of running around in a circle around Mato.

"We aren't clones silly." A small boy came and signed to him. He reminded him of a black version of Geeko. He had similar features and a similar frame. They must have been around the same age. Just a young seven-year-old boy, but this child seemed only to be interested in playing.

"What are you?" Mato asked again.

"We are perma children," the boy signed.

"Yea," the others signed. They seemed to be very proud of this fact.

"You don't look old enough to buy one of us," said a little girl. They all seemed to be dressed in male and female versions of the same blue and white uniforms.

"What's a perma child?" Mato asked. This made the little boy smile as it caused the others to line up behind him.

Galactic Mandate: The Scream

"We are children that never get old. We live our entire life in our current stage," he signed. The boy and girls moved into two lines and strutted down the middle. The moved their arms wildly and shot their hands in the air in joy. The child had to take his hand back down to be able to continue communicating with Mato. "We play here while we wait for the busy workers to come down and buy us. They bring us home, and we live in their family for the next sixty years." Suddenly all the children fell down. "Until we die," the child signed.

Mato stood there. He didn't know what to say, so he just stood there quiet, unmoving while the children picked themselves up and started to do cartwheels down the lines.

"I'm Xler. Who are you?" said the child

"My name is Mato," he replied.

"Nice to meet you. Would you like to play?"

"No. There is no time for that. I need a doctor. Do you know where I can find one? And I need to keep this quiet." Mato moved his finger to his lips making a shushing motion.

Xler looked at him confused and didn't recognize that cue.

"Your scream is terrible," he replied.

"I mean we can't tell the guards about this if they ask. This has to be our little secret. Like a spy game. Can you do that?"

"Of course. We play spy versus the league all the time. This sounds like fun," signed Xler.

Mato smiled. "There is another man here that looks like you," said the little girl that stood behind Xler.

"Thanks, Min," he signed to her.

Mato's device picked up the crosstalk.

"He does look like Mato. I bet he is a clone doctor," said Xler.

"Yes, you need a clone doctor."

"I need a Scream doctor," Mato demanded.

"Don't be silly you're a clone, and clones get clone doctors," signed Min.

"Look I can make my skin look like yours," said another little boy as he walked up to Mato. The boy switched his skin color from black to white "See?" he signed.

"That is very wonderful," Mato replied. The children all seemed to switch back and forth in unison. Sometimes they let their skin stay in black, and some seemed to prefer the opposite.

They all ran towards a central slide that was running down the middle of the room. It spiraled down and was not continuous. There seemed to be four main slides that spiraled in opposite directions to get down on every floor, and the four would make a circle as to not take up too much space. There was an automatic escalating ladder in the center that helped the children climb from one floor to the other. Mato had to use all his skills to keep up with The Scream perma children. Unlike like normal children, when it came to navigating spaces that they knew they seemed to have the best combination of speed and agility that not even Mato could match.

"Here he is," Xler signed as he pointed to a locked door that circled the birthing facility. The children all stopped and watched Mato as he moved forward.

"What's wrong?"

"That room is forbidden. And we don't want to get in trouble," Xler stated.

"Do you want to play in the water pit?" Min asked Xler.

He nodded his head, and the children were off.

"Wait!" Mato yelled, then he realized how silly that was and he laughed. "Guess I am on my own." He knocked on the door before he tried to open it. *Old habits die hard.*

"Hello," a voice asked. Mato was shocked. Someone could hear. Through the small rectangular window, Mato could see the forehead of whoever was on the other side. The tattoo was all too familiar. XXL5496 "Who is there?" the voice asked.

"I'm Mato. I'm a clone like you."

"Great another clone. Can you do me a favor? Touch the keypad. Type in up, down, 988." Mato did as he was told and this combination opened the door. Then it swung open.

"Hey kid," 96 said as he rushed past. Mato was confused by his appearance. His skin was somewhat tanned but pitch black in other places like he was one of The Scream, but as if he was stuck in mid skin transition.

"What are you?" Mato asked to his back. The man shoved shelves and what looked like vital equipment out of the way.

"Wait up," Mato demanded as the clone put on clothes from a nearby locker-room.

"Listen, kid. I know you are new at the whole being a hostage thing, but keep up," said 96.

"I'm not a hostage. I need your help. I need a doctor. The children, they said you could help," said Mato.

"Children?" 96 asked. "You mean those little old bastards. Yeah, I'm a doctor. What do you need medicine for? If you get me a ride out of here, I'll get you anything you want, kid."

"Okay, can you get me doctor?" asked Mato.

"I just told you. I am one."

Mato shook his head in disbelief.

"Look around if I wasn't a doctor why would I be here."

"I thought you said you were a hostage," said Mato.

"I can be both," said 96.

"We can't wake up Jay. We need your help."

"What, is he in cryo or something?" asked 96.

"No, he's in our pods they put us in to heal. Come I'll show you what we tried to do."

"What all this we business, are you working with The Scream?" signed 96.

"I thought you were The Scream," said Mato.

"No, I didn't get this lovely tattoo on my forehead because it looked cool. I'm a clone like you buddy."

"You seem to be a regular Elder," said Mato.

"What does that even mean kid?" said 96.

"Are you coming or not?"

Once they got to in front of the door to Mato's Room, the guard pulled him aside and tried to question him.

"Where were you and who is this?"

"He is a doctor."

"That doesn't look like a doctor, kid."

"Looks like a weird sex clone if you ask me," the other guard signed.

"This is Magistrate business. Do you want to mess with that? I'm sure he can give you demotion in no time," signed 96. The guards moved away and opened the door.

"How did you know The Magistrate told me to go find a doctor?" asked Mato.

"I didn't," 96 replied. Walking over to Jay, 96 stopped in his tracks. Memories of long ago and a planet that was far away filled his head. *Do I know him?* 96 thought. He looked at the information on the data pad and moved his hand across it. "Yes, this will take some time, but I'll wake him alright. You said The Magistrate is paying for it, correct?"

"Yes, well he ordered me to find my own doctor, that means he'll pay for one, right?" said Mato.

"No kid that means you got scammed," said 96. "I'm not going to help out your friend here until I get some payment. But I will tell you what. If you help me to retrieve something, I'll wake your friend here."

"Sure," said Mato.

"Have you ever heard of a heist?" 96 smiled.

***

Taryn was busy making a device to harness the power of the commandeered artifacts. Ulises Tom's Machine Men would work alongside her, acting as drones of Ulises's will. She needed to know more about Ulises's plan. Maybe it was not evil. Since she'd had time to think about it maybe she was overreacting to his sinister presentation. She needed to find a way to pry without revealing her intentions. "Tell me more about this beacon. I had no idea it existed. To whom do you think it will call?"

"You haven't figured it out yet? I didn't expect you to. Not anymore."

Taryn gritted her teeth.

"If you don't know I'm not going to tell you," Ulises Tom replied.

Taryn could see the red light of his eyes dim. They did not do that often. She pondered what this meant.

Taryn went on to review the designs for the devices she was making, and she noticed something about them. The beacon didn't include a message. *There is nothing to inform those on the other side what our intentions are.* This was very odd. *What could Ulises Tom be planning to do?*

Galactic Mandate: The Scream

Whom does he intend to signal? She started to ponder the possibilities. *Could there be a long-lost empire that the league no longer had contact with?* There was no way of knowing who or what could be waiting for them. She peered up at the monitors and watched a video of what must have been Ulises Tom's point of view while he scavenged through the ancient's facility. Symbols and pictures depicting great violence were shown everywhere. She surmised that Ulises Tom couldn't always control what was displayed on the monitors. Sometimes his thoughts would present memories or theories. It was hard to figure out what was from his imagination and what were memories when the video was being displayed, especially the subconscious ones.

Taryn spent hours asking questions and studying the results directly from Ulises's mind. He would display images, and she would write hidden notes of what she saw. It was a lot to go over, but she needed the information. She needed to know what evil her research was going to bring upon the galaxy.

"It's time for me to retire. Unlike you I need sleep." She complained of the long hours of research Ulises was making her do.

"Go. We will start again in six hours," said the disembodied head.

"Good enough," said Taryn. She moved back to the shuttle and eventually made her way to the space elevator for her descent back onto the planet. The calm and lonely ride gave her time to think. She thought about the formulas and equations of the current project but tried to leave it behind her. She wasn't getting enough sleep, and the doctor barely gave her any time today to catch up. The weight of it started to take effect on her eyes, and her mood was no longer steady and consistent. She began to think more of her confinement and how she would need to escape. If only Jay were awake, she would have the firepower she needed to get away.

On the way home, she realized it. *Ulises Tom doesn't know what the beacon will bring. He avoided the question at every turn. He always changes the subject.* She couldn't believe she was fooled by that quack. On the way home, she turned around. There was something more she must do. She had to go back, and she had to confront him. *This is for the galaxy; this is for science.*

"Taryn you are back. We weren't expecting you. Have you finally seen that we are the side to join?" signed The Magistrate.

"No. You are being led by a cheat. I have finally seen through his smoke and mirrors. He doesn't know what the beacon he is so enamored with will bring. He's only assuming off of pictures of destruction that there will be some kind of beast or spaceship that will come. He knows nothing and might as well place blind faith that whatever he does will work out. There is no answer to your problems, just speculation." Taryn vented her chest heaving up and down from her excitement and anger.

"I know," said The Magistrate. "We are isolated on the fringes of space. Every time we try to join the planetary league we are denied. Unable to join in the prosperity and wealth that the rest of the galaxy enjoys, my people deserve more than that. If we cannot be a part of the galaxy, then we will gladly try whatever it takes to destroy it. Ulises thinks he fools us with fancy holograms of his previous research, but we are the ones that resurrected him and keep him alive. If I weren't satisfied with his research, I wouldn't allow him to exist any longer."

Ulises' projection of his skull disappeared, and he retreated into the light of his floating head in its nutrient mix.

"I know you can't understand us. You have already rejected your people several times. But we will not be content with what the galaxy has decided for us. Join us in heart and mind. Pledge your allegiance to the goal of destroying the galaxy, and you can keep your privilege among our people."

"Never!" Taryn interrupted.

"You struggle to try and save something that is doomed. If there is one thing The Scream is good at, it's destruction. Everything you know will eventually fall by the wave of my hand," signed The Magistrate.

Taryn frowned then grabbed a plasma soldering iron. She thrust it forward and tried to catch The Magistrate off-guard, but he moved around and dodged her, clicking a button on his shirt. The lights flashed red, and the floor vibrated.

"Machine Men come to me. It's an emergency."

Ulises Tom's projection turned back on. The projected mouth seemed to be screaming for help.

The Machine Men guards rushed in and tried to subdue Taryn. They came from behind her. She swung her soldering iron at them, and they were forced to proceed to with caution. A guard tried to punch her and learned that the soldering iron could melt his arm off quickly when it was turned to its highest setting. He backed away. It seemed he was not used to being physically threatened by a biological being. A quick flick by the other guard and she was out. The fight with the first had made her distracted, and she didn't realize the other guard had snuck around and had gotten behind her. He had a direct shot and used his solid metal fingers to flick the back of her head creating a popping sound. Taryn fell to the floor.

"Take her away. She will learn the hard way that she should have joined her people," The Magistrate signed.

Chapter 16

96 stood as a lookout. He looked up and down the hallway, moving around and trying to cover both directions as much as possible. He could not rely on his hearing anymore to cover his blind spots, so he had to make sure there were none.

"It's all clear Mato," he signed, then pushing the young man up into a vent above a locked door.

"This looks like someone's room," said Mato. He made sure to turn his head so 96 could see the translation. They were in a small hallway filled with a door, and windows to the outside and not much else. The walls were mostly grey and black plastic, and the setting seemed very much like a spaceship.

"Just get in and steal what's inside. It's a sonic disruptor, and you should know it when you see it. They told me it is the most powerful in the galaxy," signed 96.

"OK," Mato replied, removing the small vent cover. He progressed forward, worried that he might get stuck in the minimal space. If he were just a kilogram or two bigger, he would have. He nudged and moved until he got to the other side.

On the other side, he found nothing that looked like a disrupter. Mostly ornate things that looked like they were made of expensive metals, and crystals, even some models of what had to be places that existed across the galaxy. He walked over to a private computer system that had a tape deck and a rectangular table with a large protruding head that said "Snuff films." He recognized what was going on here. *This is just a burglary. There is no disrupter here.* Time to grab everything that he could find of any unique value. Mato filled a backpack he found with valuables and tapes. Not just the one that said snuff but the ones that said "experiment" and "hidden." *Whatever these are they must be valuable to someone.* 96 must think he was an idiot because he grew up on the reservation. Mato would show him. The valuables were loaded into the backpack as tightly as he could get them. He heard a knock on the door. That was the signal someone was coming, and he had to get going. Mato finished up then opened the door from the inside, causing a visual alarm to go off. Lights changed color and the floor vibrated with a pulsing. 96 signed that it was time to go.

"How are we going to get this stuff past the guards?" Mato asked, showing 96 a brief preview of what he had stolen.

"We will find a way," 96 replied. They rushed down the hallway. A concerned citizen spotted them and must have signaled guards to come because they were right behind them.

The guards ran after them, and 96 instinctively yelled. "We have to split up!" just before they found a small nook to hide in. They watched as the guards ran past them. The tone of the voice was out of pitch, and it was a type of voice Mato had never heard before. He knew that 96 was deaf but couldn't explain the voice that came from him. He had never experienced something like that before.

"Give me the stuff, and I'll go left while you go right." 96 signed.

"No way," Mato replied.

"Listen, if we don't figure it out now, we will both be caught, and I don't think we will have guest room privileges anymore. The Scream can be a very mean people," signed 96.

"Fine, you can have these tapes, but I am keeping the rest," said Mato.

"Do it quickly."

Mato opened up the back page and flung the tapes at him, throwing one too hard. It slipped past their hiding spot and into the main hallway. 96 rushed after it.

Guards saw this and were waiting upon 96's exit. Mato balled up his fist and was ready to fight his way out of the situation. He was still hidden, so he didn't reveal himself, waiting for the time to be right. He couldn't see the conversation that 96 was having and there nothing but the most incidental of sounds.

"So, you broke into Villa Don's apartment for what reason?" the guards questioned.

"He had something I needed," 96 signed.

"No more shenanigans from you. I told Doctor Don that this was going to be a failed experiment. You seem to be having a hard time adjusting to Scream Society. We should lock you away and throw away the vibrate."

"Let's just do that." The lights switched back to normal, and the floor stopped pulsating. The alarm was now turned off. They restrained 96 with maglocks and pushed and shoved him towards the hall.

"You're not going to the doctor this time. I think a few nights in jail should do you good," signed the guards.

The firm footsteps of the guards and the sporadic step of 96 could be heard by Mato as they shoved him back into the main hallways. *There must have been something I missed if they went through all this trouble to capture us.* After stashing the stolen items in the nook that he had found behind a wall panel, Mato headed back to the apartment. *I must go and see if there is anything else. Maybe there was a disrupter there or something else that was really important.* He'd have to go investigate this on his own now. That meant he'd have to be extra careful. Sneaking past the average citizens that were going about their day, Mato found that he was in luck. The door was still open, and the alarm was off. He no longer needed to worry about it going off and bringing the guards back. Making his way back into the rooms he was shocked to see a man standing there as if he was waiting for him. Turning around the man started to move his hands.

"Criminals always return to the scene of the crime," he signed. A wave of panic filled Mato as he looked for the door. It shut after his entrance, and he was trapped inside.

"Criminal, I am no criminal. Look I don't have any of your stuff," he replied.

"Cut the crap. I know it was you, and probably my clone friend 96. Did he promise you a share of the cut?"

"No," Mato replied, surprising himself because it was truly an honest answer.

"Listen you look like a decent young clone with your whole life ahead of you. You don't want to be caught up in the mess 96 is leaving," said the man.

"Who are you?" asked Mato.

"I'm a doctor."

"If I help you can you help me?" asked Mato.

"Yes, I might need you to do something your friends might not agree with. Can you handle that clone?"

"Only if you can wake Jay. No one has been able to do it. If you can't do that then no deal."

"Trust me, waking your friend should be no problem. I will just need you to put this device in 96's clothing. It's very small and nearly untraceable. I know he will escape again. He has done it several times. Do you think that is a fair price to wake up your friend?" said the doctor.

"Is it a tracking device?" asked Mato.

"No, nothing so simple. I already got several of those placed on him, but this one will do what the other can't."

"What's that?"

"It will stun him, rendering him awake, but unable to move."

"That doesn't sound right."

"It will help me capture him for the final time. And it is the price you will have to pay. How much is this Jay worth to you?"

"Clones don't betray clones," said Mato.

"We both know that is not true. If it were, Skyfall would not have been the instrument of your civilization's destruction."

Mato reached out his hand and grabbed the small blue device from the doctor. It glowed slightly and seemed rather hard to hide. When he ran his fingers over it, it came apart revealing a remote trigger. The doctor nodded his head. Mato stared up and lifted his head quickly in agreement.

"Let me show you to our room is so you can help Jay," said Mato.

***

The doctor looked over the datapad. He moved his fingers revealing hidden menus. "Someone has been messing with the software. They thought this was a purely technical issue. Pity, if they knew just a little bit more about biology, they would have had it," the doctor signed to Mato.

"I don't care," he replied.

"Of course, you don't, this is the wondering of the scientific mind my boy," the doctor signed back.

"Just fix him."

"Oh no, I won't just fix him. I will make him better. You see, we need to balance out his hormones, give him a few stimulants," the doctor continued. He was signing with his left hand while he typed on the datapad on the other. Mato was slightly impressed; it was the first time he saw someone do this. The default voice of his translation device changed ever so slightly to indicate a slang or accent as Mato could tell.

"Why isn't it working? I thought you were a good doctor," Mato asked.

"Patience. Unlike whoever your technologic friend is, who must have promised instant results, these things take time. But I do have one way to speed it up. Would you like me to try? It might hurt him a little bit. Just a tiny bit I mean," signed the doctor in his accented language.

"Do it. We need him," said Mato.

"Starting electroshock waking process now."

Cables dropped down from the ceiling and attached themselves to Jay. The doctor smiled and his screened turned into one large button that he could press. After preparing Jay's body for the process, he was going to put him in. He injected a small vial into his blood.

"This will make sure the procedure is more effective," signed the doctor. He sat down in a chair directly across from Jay and warned Mato. "Make sure not to touch him once I begin. You might get hurt."

"Get hurt? Wait what are you going to do?" asked Mato.

The doctor pressed the large button on his screen, and immediately the subtle hiss of electricity was heard by Mato and Jay's body started to convulse.

"Again," the doctor signed.

Jay was hit with another round of electric shock.

"Oh, he is a strong one. Let's turn it up," signed the doctor as he turned the dial on the button that appeared on his screen. Jay's body convulsed, and his eyes were now wide open, but there was no life behind them. Mato ran to him. "Remember, don't touch," signed the doctor who then the hit the button again, starting the shock all over. Jay's brown eyes suddenly had life as he screamed out.

"Who???" he asked.

Mato celebrated shouting and hollering. "Welcome back!!" he yelled.

Jay reached out and punched the kid right in his helmet, snatching it from Mato's head and ripping the connections from his body at the same time. He threw the helmet up and used the hand as a bat to spike the helmet directly at the doctor who didn't have time to shield himself. He took the full force of the hit, knocking the wind out of him.

"Jay wait! He was helping you," said Mato.

"And I was just thanking him." Jay studied the doctor, looking at him up and down. Then he studied the room and looked over at the wall and the door. His eyes moved back to the doctor whose hands moving in coordinated signs that he didn't understand.

"Don't tell me we actually are in Silent Space," said Jay.

"Yes, we have been here for almost two weeks now," replied Mato. He rubbed the side of his head that took the punch.

"These color changing bastards diddle you?" he asked.

Mato shook his head.

"Good. Where is Taryn?" he asked in a demanding manner.

"She is still on the ship. She should have been here by now, but they make her work a lot in some lab. She says it's an advancement of her project and she doesn't want me to come to bother or embarrass her," said Mato.

"She needs to be rescued then."

"No, she comes back every day to sleep then heads out again in the morning."

"She is getting rescued whether she likes it or not," said Jay.

"What is this color changing bastard trying to tell us?"

"I don't know you took my translation helmet and beat him with it."

"So that's what the silly looking thing on your head was?"

"I need it to understand them. You will need one, too, if you're going to communicate."

"The hell I will. The Scream will get what I am saying without one of those funny looking helmets, just ask the doctor," said Jay. He picked up the helmet and put it back on Mato's head. The main screen was cracked, but the helmet still displayed symbols. "Ask the doctor if he needs me to wear a helmet or does he understand?" said Jay.

"I don't know if it's working or not."

"Well ask, and you'll find out," said Jay.

"Doctor Don. Jay wants to know if you understand him," said Mato as he looked directly at the doctor. His screen still updated but it was a little slower, and he had to talk just a bit more carefully for it to catch everything.

"Tell Jay he's an asshole and I know how to read lips," the doctor signed. Mato relayed the information to Jay who laughed then smiled.

"Tell the doctor he's right."

Mato again relayed the information.

The doctor looked up and signed. "Remember our deal." Mato opened his hand releasing the device and nodded.

"Time to get some guns," Jay announced. He pressed the button and opened the door. The guard's stationed outside of it looked very surprised. They pressed a button calling for backup, but it was already too late for them. Moving quickly and with purpose, Jay smacked both of their heads together, their helmets clanking and pinging. Civilians who saw this turned and went in the opposite direction. They fell to the floor, and he grabbed their weapons shooting both guards for good measure. The weapons hit with a very long bass sound. The force from the sonic blast lifted him up from the ground each time he fired the weapon. "I might just keep this," Jay said, leading Mato out of the room.

The doctor did not get up from his crouched and prone position. He signed "You are better than this," to Mato as they left the room.

"Jay where are we going?" said Mato.

"I was just about to ask you the same thing. Show me where that ship is, and we're there," said Jay.

"It's that way, but we have to get in a giant elevator. There is no way to just spring her out."

"You leave that to me. All I need you to do is point the direction, OK? I'm a professional at this. Before she knows it, she will be saved," said Jay.

Jay started running through the crowd of people with Mato running close behind. He pushed those who couldn't move in time. They looked at him and tried to sign messages, but Jay looked back and wasn't interested. He raised his gun, and they stopped signing and moved. Running down a long corridor, the bass sound of sonic blasts followed them as they ran. The backup the initial guards had called for arrived. On jet assisted horizontal flight they tried to catch up, and they did so rapidly. Throwing Mato a gun, Jay fired behind him. The bass filled shot whipped past Mato, and they rushed past in a hurry. The guards stopped their assisted chase when Jay's unaided shots kept hitting random civilians. They tumbled and were ripped in half by the sonic weapons. After three people died in the crossfire, the guards gave up and stopped their pursuit.

One of the guards opened up a link on his armband. It instantly connected to the battleship above. With one hand he gave hand signs which must have indicated the situation and the entire base went on high alert. Lights were flashing yellow and red colors while Jay and Mato ran down the long corridor to the space elevator. The civilians cleared a path and Jay no longer had to push and shove his way past the crowd. At the end of the long corridor stood the door to the space elevator. Workers were loading on supplies that were apparently needed by the ship, then they turned around because of Jay's approach. They ran out of the way while the guards started shooting. These guards were different from before. They guarded the entrance with their lives and didn't stop at the sight of civilian casualties. They continued to fire as people got in the way of their shots. They exploded, and Jay didn't move. He didn't run to duck or hide; he slowly walked towards the guards. They fired and fired quickly, overheating their weapons. Once the crowd and the workers were out of the way, Jay opened fire. The armor the guards wore kept them from exploding on contact with jay's sonic weapon, but they were flung to the back of the room by the elevator. Badly injured, they were left spitting up blood in the corner.

"This is easier than I thought," Jay muttered. Grabbing one of the workers, he dragged the young man who wore an orange jumpsuit to the controls. Jay sneered with his eyes. He tried to say everything that he needed with a look, and he did. The man started to punch in codes and turned a key.

"Activate the elevator," Mato demanded redundantly. Once the elevator started moving Jay threw the worker out the doors. He got up and ran away. They were off to the spaceship.

Fighters were deployed, and as Jay and Mato ascended with the elevator, they circled it and watched. They gave every indication that if anything was wrong, they could disintegrate the elevator and its two passengers without a second thought.

"Why haven't they shot us yet," asked Mato.

"It's all about money. Simply, it would cost too much. They don't want to splatter our brains because they would have to build a new elevator. I've been in their shoes before, and as long as we don't make any indication that we have a bomb we're good," said Jay. "You're a little fighter, aren't you?" Jay asked.

"Yea on the res. I saved Eyota's butt a couple of times. I was known to scrap as well."

"I bet you were. Have you given any thought to what you are going to do after this?" said Jay.

"What do you mean?"

"Eventually this mission will be over, and you're not a member of my team so I can't pay you, but you could be. You are definitely better than the people I brought with me."

"Are you sure you want a clone on your team?" asked Mato.

"As long as you don't give me trouble when we work for The Acolytes, yea. I don't care about your upbringing as long as you can kick ass," said Jay.

"The ship, it's coming up," Mato replied. They braced themselves as the fighters flew away. Soon they were inside the ship, and a welcoming committee of guards was prepared to shred the interior of the elevator. Jay moved the boxes in the way to provide some cover. "I'm not going to lie, this is going to get hairy quick," said Jay.

"I'm no late model. I can handle this."

"Sure, whatever that means," said Jay.

The door opened, and the firing started immediately. Jay's ears rang from all the sonic blasts that were happening around him. Mato was happy that his helmet came with some noise cancellation and he wasn't assaulted by all the low- and high-pitched noises that were occurring around them. Jay methodically killed the more immediate threats then moved the show onto those who were in the back. His shots were dead on, and he didn't miss a single one. The ship's captain who led the assault grew nervous and tried to move farther and farther away from the entrance. He opened up his armband assistant and started to sign for more guards, but his hand was grabbed by Jay. The soldiers in the elevator room were already defeated.

"Where is my girlfriend?" Jay demanded.

"I may be young, but even I know she is not your girlfriend," said Mato.

"I said, where is she?" Jay demanded, gripping the captain's face and squeezing.

"Unlike me, you don't need your mouth to talk. So, I would sign the correct information before I rip out your jaw," demanded Jay.

"He can't understand you," said Mato.

Mato looked the captain in his glowing purple eyes. "We need to know where the scientist Taryn is. Tell us now," Mato demanded. The captain nodded.

"I'll break your hands if you lie," Jay yelled.

The captain didn't bother with signing the details but pointed to a shuttle that resided about fifty meters away. Grabbing the captain and putting his hand behind his back, they moved to the shuttle. The captain cried. Mato was shaken. He had never seen a person with a position of this much power cry before.

"Why are you crying? You should man up," said Mato.

The captain moved his head to the left and looked at down at where his hand should be. Mato noticed that his hand was cuffed behind his back and the man couldn't communicate or reply to his question.

"If I move your cuffs to the front, I don't want any of that funny business. OK?"

The captain nodded in agreement. Mato uncuffed the captain, and he did not show any act of aggression. He waited for the young man to re-cuff him in front. Mato looked down at the captain's hands and stared at his crotch. This made him uncomfortable, but the awkward stare had to be done if he wanted the captain to communicate with him.

"Thank you, young man. Handcuffing one of The Scream behind our backs is the ultimate sign of disrespect because he can no longer communicate with the outside world. It is actually what we use for torture," the captain signed.

"I didn't know that," Mato replied.

"No one seems to. That is why we prefer not to get captured in battle. It's best to be dead than unable to sign anything. I will remember this, young man," said the captain.

The short trip to the laboratory was already over. They moved out of the shuttle and were on the specially built landing platform.

"That's strange," the captain signed. There were no guards, and the door to the lab was open.

"You are a primate in a state-of-the-art lab. There is no harm you can cause here," said Ulises Tom.

"Well ain't that a nice way to welcome Death's Witness. Ulises Tom, I presume?" said Jay.

Mato looked around and saw that the lab workers and all the guards were gone. There was no one there beside the strange floating head that talked.

"If you are looking for Taryn, I assume they are torturing her as we speak," said Ulises Tom.

"Now I have heard of you. You were lucky they only sent black ops after you all those years ago. Death's Witness would have killed you, and they would have done it right. You wouldn't be a floating head, that is for sure," said Jay.

"Like the others, you are a fool." Then Jay disintegrated the tank. Nutrient-filled water splashed everywhere.

"From what I read in his file that guy had a mouth on him. We would be here all cycle if I hadn't have done that," said Jay. Mato recognized what he saw on the table, what looked to be his artifact and the others that were just like it. He reached and grabbed all three artifacts that he could find, putting them inside his shirt. Jay grabbed the captain. He raised his gun and pointed it directly at the middle of his chest. The captain puffed it out and stood defiantly.

"Wait!" demanded Mato.

"You better have a good reason for saving him. He is the enemy here."

"Maybe, but let me speak with him. "

"You have thirty seconds to get the truth out of him, or I shoot. I don't care if you are in the way boy," said Jay.

"Where is Taryn?" Mato asked.

"I don't know," The captain replied.

"I can't save you." Mato put his head down. Jay raised his gun and was about to fire.

"Looks like he remembered something," said Jay.

Mato put his head up and pointed his helmet at the captain's hands. "He says she might be in the brig. We should check there." Mato relayed.

Jay grabbed him and pushed him forward, back toward the shuttle from which they had come. The captain's hands were turned forward and could switch back to speak to Mato. He tried to make eye contact, but Mato shied away.

"Move," Jay demanded.

"He can't hear you."

"But he understands," Jay replied. Getting back in the shuttle and closing the shuttle door behind them. Jay asked, "How do we get to the brig?"

"He says we should have asked sooner? We can't get to it from the shuttle. It's in the lower decks by the engine."

"Well, they aren't going to like what I have to say about that." Jay took command of the shuttle and started piloting towards the back of the ship. He came upon a wall spanning the rear end of the ship. He was unable to fly through and had to land to get anywhere. He primed the weapons system. This started the alarms of the ship all over again. Lights went off, and they went out in unique sequences that neither Jay or Mato had seen before. They seemed to be conveying a message with each flash of the changing color.

"Good thing. I thought The Scream had gone to sleep after I kicked the welcoming party's ass," said Jay. He typed in commands and moved dials. Two joysticks popped out of the dash of the shuttle, but Jay moved them together until they were touching.

"What does that do?" Mato asked.

"We are in drilling mode," Jay replied. He pulled the trigger, firing the large sonic cannon housed on the shuttle. It drew a lot of attention. Internal lasers started to fire, and soldiers on the ground engaged the ship. The drill pulsed and made an inverted bass sound as it shredded the metal wall and ship corridor. The metal folded in on itself as the shuttle drill cleared a path for its descent into the ship. With the lasers, sonic weapons and stray fire that was coming in, Jay didn't wait for the drill to make a lot of progress.

"What are you doing?" Mato asked.

"Brace yourself. We can't wait for the drill to do its thing. We have to put it right in their butts," said Jay. Mato frowned. The shuttle slammed into the parent ship, and the crew was thrown against the walls of the shuttle. Mato complained of how it hurt while the ship captain was knocked unconscious.

"He's not going to be telling us any more directions," said Jay. He picked up Mato and opened the shuttle doors. *Lucky son of a bitch. The door isn't jammed.* Jumping out he made his way to the back of the ship.

The Scream took pride in properly labeling their warship. It was easy to find everything by looking up at the directions and looking for pointer arrows. If you were in the right areas, you didn't need to stop and ask where you were going. This helped Jay find which direction he needed to go. Mato got up. He held a sonic rifle and looked like he was born to fight now. He shot any transgressor to dared cross paths with him and Jay. Bursting into the brig area, Jay surprised The Magistrate who's back was turned. He had been enjoying the sight of Taryn as they hit her with wave after wave of a sonic blaster. They were gentler than the weaponized version but were made to annoy and torture, not kill.

"Who are you?" The Magistrate signed.

"I don't have time for this," Jay replied, leading with a commanding punch to the face. Knocking The Magistrate out, he threw him over his shoulder and went to open Taryn's restraints.

"Thank you," said Taryn, her voice weak from the torture. She had screamed when they hit her with the sonic waves, but The Scream couldn't hear her, so it made no difference. They made no attempt at muting her cries, which only made them worse.

"Come on. We need to get to some escape pods."

"Wait," said Mato. He was standing by the restrained body of 96 who made pleas to help him. His hands and legs were tied up vertically on the restraining table as he tried to resist and make noise so that anyone who would pass by would notice him. "I know him. He helped me find the doctor that woke you up," said Mato.

"Well, thanks for the good deed. We are not taking him with us."

"But you owe him," said Mato.

"No, I don't, and neither do you. If he found himself in this mess, he will figure a way out."

"The way you and Taryn figured out how to wake yourselves up? You would be stuck with no way to get out. What if he said the same thing while you were asleep and no one could wake you up?"

"All right but you are responsible for him."

"Thank you," 96 said in his out of pitch voice.

"Come on we have to get to the escape pods," said Mato.

"Do you have our loot?" 96 signed.

"What?" Mato replied, leaving towards the hole in the door Jay created. The group fired their sonic weapons hitting anyone they could find. The soldier rushed them in the hallways, but Jay hit the control of a door and locked them out to the escape pod room. He placed The Magistrate in an escape pod and launched it. Then he launched several of the others.

"OK, there is just enough left for us now. With their leader being in a pod they won't dare shoot them down."

"How will they know?"

"Trust me they are watching."

They got in the remaining escape pods and launched as well, heading for the planet below. Fighters were launched, but they seemed to be searching for their lost leader. They did not pay attention to Jay's pod which he occupied with Taryn. They didn't pay attention to Mato's pod which he held with 96. Some of the empty pods were destroyed, but by the time they got to the planet, only a few were damaged. The Scream now searched for their missing leader as much as they search for Jay and his group of fugitives.

Chapter 17

They crashed landed in a field. Jay's and Mato's pods crashed within 300 meters of each other, and the clear rocky planet fields made it easy to see each other. Jay opened his pod door and surveyed the land. "You know, the ride down wasn't so bad. Maybe we should share a pod again," said Jay.

"In your dreams... Maybe mine as well," said Taryn. Jay perked up and straightened his back. He wore a smile on his face, and he held his sonic rifle up. He waved it for the others to come and join him.

Looking around, Jay saw a house and a vast greenhouse operation. The house was odd as it was round and rocky, perhaps to blend in with the natural landscape.

"We will need to get out of here as soon as possible. The authorities won't take too long to find our crash site.

"That greenhouse should have some large trucks that we can get on and find a spaceport."

"Are you sure that will work? The Scream isn't known for their busy spaceports and tourists from other empires coming and going. We are going to stand out wherever we go," said Taryn.

Mato nodded his head in agreement.

"It's not ideal, but you have to go wherever the mission takes you and right now this is where the mission is taking us," said Jay.

Jay started running, his body hunched over to keep a low profile, and the rest of his group followed suit. They rushed to the greenhouse walls. They hide behind various fruit trees and vegetable plants. The greenhouse seemed to house the standard variety of fruits and vegetables for the planet. From what the group could tell, the operation was nothing special, just food for the population. Workers were tending to giant machines that handled most of the plants of the greenhouse, and they were loading vegetables on the trucks and offloading empty boxes.

"Odd they don't seem to be on high alert," Jay whispered.

"They can't hear anything remember," Mato replied.

"Lucky for us," said Jay.

A worker started to look in their direction. He signed to his co-workers something that Jay could not understand. Mato raised his gun and pushed it forward in the bush which he was hiding.

"Wait!" Jay called out.

Mato looked confused. His eyebrows were pushed together, and he gave the impression that he was awaiting an answer.

"The less confrontation, the better right now. We can't leave too easy of a trail for The Scream to follow," said Jay.

"That's smart," Mato replied, and Taryn rolled her eyes.

96 looked at Jay and stared at Mato hoping he would turn his head and so he could see the translation on his helmet. Being in the back of the group he didn't quite know what was going on. He had to watch and be alert. If something terrible happened, he was aware that he would be the last to know.

Taryn was hiding on Jay's right and looking intensely at the truck. She was looking over its mechanics and pondered what kind of computer system it had. If it was universal enough, she should be able to hijack its programming. She knew that they would just be hitching a ride, but she wanted to stay a step ahead. She realized that being the most technical of the bunch, they would call on her if they ran into any problems.

The workers pointed and started walking in their direction. The group became very nervous. Jay held out his hand and tried to keep everyone calm. "Not yet," he reminded them. A sizeable metallic tower that the worker was moving towards spun awake. Its mechanical arms stamped something on the worker's hand, and they all changed direction and went towards the house, away from the group.

As soon as the workers were no longer in direct sight, Jay ordered, "Hurry up, we are not going to get another opening like this." The group ran towards the truck. It hovered gracefully with an open top. It had several boxes and a tarp that the workers used to protect the produce while it was in transit. Jay stood at the bottom and held his hands out, helping the others climb in. Taryn went first, then Mato, and last 96. Jay grabbed on to the rugged sides of the truck and lifted himself, grunting as he did it. Mato and 96 reached out over the edge and grabbed his arms, providing some support as he climbed over.

"I'm going in front to hijack the truck," said Taryn.

"You can't do that. It will be too obvious and easy to track us," said Jay

"They won't track my work. I'm one of the best in the galaxy."

"They won't have to. It's a fucking truck. It will be obvious it's missing. If you want to help, find out where this truck is headed then report back."

"Sure, just remember I'm not the soldier, you can't just order me around. In fact, I hired you. You work for me."

"We are way beyond that," said Jay.

Taryn raised an eyebrow. She moved her head back and stared at him for a second. Jay could almost see the thoughts running through her head. She turned around a walked to the front of the truck. She opened the door to the cabin. Soon she returned. The others helped fix the tarp and the hiding spots. Jay pointed to places he wanted things to be moved, and they instinctively knew what to do. He didn't dish out any verbal command, but he didn't need to. Their fates were tied together, and he was the most experienced of the group. They listened to what Jay wanted. They watched his reactions and followed his cues. Jay thought about the group. For a client and a group of tag alongs, they were doing ok. He would prefer to have a well-trained team from back in his military days, but this group was the next best thing. Well maybe not the next best thing, but they were what he had.

"It's headed to some kind of train station."

"That is great," Jay stated. "We will be able to hop a train to a spaceport in no time."

"Is this the best course of action to take?" Taryn asked.

"For right now yes. Our first priority is to get a ship and get out of here. Preferably one that can get out of here unnoticed."

"What are these symbols?" Taryn asked. She looked amazed at some markings that were spray painted on the inside of the truck.

"Those are gang signs," Mato replied.

Galactic Mandate: The Scream

Taryn's eyes grew wide, and she looked around with sudden alarm. "How would you know? You didn't grow up on this planet. "

"Now but I grew up on the res, and we had plenty of gangs back there."

"I think the kid is right," said Jay.

Mato felt a tapping on his shoulder. It was 96, and he almost turned Mato around. He signed a message, and Mato leaned over and relayed. "He is saying something about a gang of rejected perma children. He says they are not to be messed with."

Jay readied his sonic weapon and looked at the room. "I hope they show up. Keep things interesting."

"I thought you just said we are trying to keep a low profile," said Taryn

"Keeping a low profile is the best way to hide. Well, second only to causing chaos," said Jay.

The group heard the strange whizzing sound of the machine as it stamped the returning workers. Jay and his group returned to their hiding spots. Jay tried to listen for sounds of a conversation. *I forgot they all talk with their hands. There is no way to know if they are on to us.* He readied his weapon, and he looked over at 96 who was stiff as a board. His only focus seemed to be hiding well and staying out of sight. His eyes moved to Mato who was watching him. They locked eyes, and Mato readied his sonic rifle as well. Jay shook his head, ordering the young clone to stand down. Then he checked on Taryn. Her gazed seem to be only on the front of the truck, at the door that led to the cabin. She stared at it so intensely her eyes could burn a hole through it. She watched and was almost knocked off her feet when the truck started to move. The hovering vehicle raised itself to be even higher than it was when they had climbed in. The ground felt uneasy below them as the truck shook and bounced up and down according to the road on which they traveled. The truck accelerated and got to cruising speed. They were off to their next destination, and there was no fight. Jay wiped the sweat from his brow and relaxed. The rest of the group followed suit.

It was several hours before the vehicle came to a stop. The hot sun of the day descended and the cold night began. The group shivered and whimpered because none were clothed correctly for the occasion. The truck lowered itself to the ground, and the group could hear the sound of the workers leaving the front cabin. The group could hear their footsteps, as they slowly walked away from the truck.

"I think we are here," whispered Mato.

"We better be," whispered Jay.

"Why haven't they unloaded this truck yet?" asked Taryn.

96 signed something, but Jay assumed it was unimportant from the way 96 looked at Mato. Jay could tell that 96 duplicated what Taryn had said.

"I'll check it out," said Jay.

He climbed up on a box and stood on his toes to look over the side of the truck. The truck was parked right outside of the train yard. But a group of strangely dressed Scream women surrounded them. They all wore masks made out of mirrored bulbs, and each one had a sonic weapon. The mask that they wore displayed hand signs in the Scream's language. Jay was trying to figure out the unique sight that was before him. He realized that he could hear this group or gang as they spoke. They were speaking.

"What's going on out there? Me and 96 want to know," said Mato. Jay looked back and shushed him. Jay could see Taryn on his left. She looked like she had a question as well, but she held it. Jay stood back on his toes and looked over the side again. Much to his surprise, there was another group that approached. They were dressed in monochromic tan colored uniforms. They also wore masks mixed with feathers on their necks. It gave them a huge presence that each member commanded. Their masks were a brass color that shined against the building lights of the train station. When they spoke hand signs would appear in place of their eyes to translate what they were saying. Jay turned his head so that he could listen to what was being said.

"The station belongs to us the Chosen Children. Get out of here, or there is going to be some problems, little girls," said their leader.

The leader of the other gang smacked the workers, and they ran off. They appeared to run out into the darkness making a line down the middle of where the two gangs were challenging each other.

"The Cloud Sisters will not back down. We already went over this. We got the train station and the casinos, and Chosen Children are supposed to stay with your craft pod racers."

Galactic Mandate: The Scream

"Craft pods. No one wants to see that anymore. It's old, decades old, and we need a new gig, so I'm taking yours," said the tall figure with the brass mask. He touched a button on its side, and the mask unlocked, and it flipped up above his head like a visor. The leader of the Cloud Sisters took off her helmet too. She lifted it up and held it just above her waist.

"We don't want any trouble. We are just collecting our due taxes. Let's work something out." Jay could see that she was using the helmet as a distraction as she had what looked like a handheld sonic gun behind her back.

"See that's not going to work. The Chosen Children don't share. We don't have to," the man replied.

Jay ducked back down under the tarp. "What is going on out there?" Taryn asked.

"They are about to shoot up the place," Jay replied.

Mato readied his sonic blaster. "I'm ready," he stated.

"Not yet. We wait for them to kill each other, then we wallop them after," Jay commanded. He looked around to verify that they understood the commands. They all had a serious glare on their faces. "I'm really going to enjoy this," Jay whispered. He motioned to Mato that once he was ready, he would lift him up and over the top.

"Can I have your rifle?" asked Mato.

"Why?"

"I like it better with two."

"You know kid, you are all right. I got to have you join my team when all this is said and done. But you can't have my gun. A soldier never loans out his only weapon. That is your first lesson." Jay lifted himself back up to monitor the situation outside.

"How dare you!" shouted the leader of the Cloud Sisters. She moved her hand from her backside and shot her sonic blast at her rival. He dodged and was able to run out of the way in time to avoid behind caught by the surprise attack. His mask went down, and the rest of his gang raised their hidden weapons. The two groups opened fire on each other. The gang members stood out in the open and shot in line at each other. They didn't move to the sides or duck aside from the leader of the Chosen Children. He moved to the sides and ducked in between his men. The gangsters were knocked over one by one from the sonic weapons. They looked like pins falling individually.

The distinct bass sound of sonic weapons hit reverberated against the back of the truck. The group had to cover their eyes as it was making them dizzy from all the swoops and popping sounds that were being made outside.

The Cloud Sisters fired but were quickly outgunned by the Chosen Children with their bold stance and unrelenting attack. Soon it was their leader who found herself alone, surrounded by dead bodies. The last Cloud Sister held her guns out for the other to see. She kept her arms straight and spread. She had her fingers on the trigger and stared down the rival gang members who stopped firing once it was just her left. The leader of the Chosen Children returned. Not only did they take the train station but they did it in style.

"That was quicker than I thought." Jay had seen enough. He laughed to himself at the imposter techniques used by the gangsters. If it were him in his prime, he could waste both groups without breaking a sweat. Those days were long over, but he knew that the gangsters would be no match for him. *Wonder what the kid will do. He has so much heartache, reminds me of myself when I was younger,* Jay thought of Mato. *I should test him to see what he can do here.*

"Ok youngster you're up," said Jay.

The other lifted the tarp and moved it backward. Jay locked his hands together creating a fake step. Mato smiled; he knew precisely what had to be done. He ran forward and jumped, letting his foot fall into Jay's hands. The older soldier pushed and lifted him as far as he could, throwing the young one over the edge of the wall of the produce truck. Mato rolled on his side as he landed making a loud slapping noise. The gangsters who were watching their surroundings were alerted by Mato's presence and suddenly focused all their attention towards the boy.

"Who are you?" asked the leader of the Chosen Children. He did not wait for a response. He pointed and ordered his men to "Get him!" The swopping sound of sonic weapons made their annoying bass noise as Mato tried to return fire. His rifle was damaged in his jump and wouldn't fire. He pulled the trigger, and it made a clicking noise, but no sonic wave came out. Mato looked back at Jay, and he panicked and had to run away. He turned and ran towards the side of the truck. The leader of the Cloud Sisters got up and took her guns while the others were distracted and fired her guns into the backs of the distracted Chosen Children. With one shot she killed the stray gangster that was closest to her. Her sonic weapon blew his arm off, ripping it from its socket leaving a broken man on the ground bleeding from his wounds. He fell on top of one of her soldier's mangled bodies making a bloody mess of two people's clashing body parts. The Cloud Sister fired again and killed the next closest gangster, ripping a hole in his midsection. The man grabbed at the missing region while he fell to the ground and screamed out. A second later his body was lifeless. The Cloud Sister aimed at the next target only to have her weapon knocked away.

The Cloud Sister's rival, the leader of the Chosen Children, punched and kicked her. He swatted her arms and grabbed for her gun. She locked her arms, and they embraced in a struggle for the weapon. The larger man pushed and shoved her, and he tried to use his weight to his advantage. He leaned heavily on her and slowly worked on her grip. She could feel her hands getting looser and the sweat on her palms working against her. He jabbed her with his elbow, and they tumbled to the ground.

Jay watched as the young Mato ran towards him. He had his rifle at the ready. He wanted to intervene but decide that a test would not be a test without the young one learning to deal with impossible situations on his own.

"What are you doing standing there? Help him," shouted Taryn.

"He will figure it out, trust me," Jay rebutted.

The sound of their voices was loud enough that without the tarp to muffle it during the fighting the Chosen Children could hear. The ones closest raised their eyebrows in curiosity and that quick second of distraction was all that Mato needed to double back and get them engaged in a fist fight. He came in and punched hard, smacking one of the Children in his bronze mask. The smack surprised him and got him off balance. The other gangster that was to his left fired at the ground, missing Mato and catching his fellow gangster's leg, tearing into it. The gangster screamed, causing the one on the left to stop firing. A big mistake. Mato got low to the ground and swept his legs. The gangster fell over, dropping his weapon. Mato grabbed it and knocked both the gangsters quickly in the head with the butt of the gun.

With a new weapon in hand, Mato fired quickly and divisively, finishing off all the remaining gangsters before they could react. The only two that were left were their leaders, the leader of the Cloud Sisters and the leader of the Chosen Children. The brass faced man had wrested control of the gun from his rival. He stood over her and watched her frown at him. She didn't want to appear weak. The leader of the Chosen Children held his sonic pistol aimed at the other leader's head. He smiled almost uncontrollably.

"Do you have any idea how much you have cost me?" he asked her.

She did not respond. She moved backward to put some space between her and her attacker. Mato had seen enough. He didn't need to know anymore. He held up his rifle and blaster the Chosen Children leader, shredding him in half. The Cloud Sister had a shocked look on her face. Blood was spilled all over her. She tried to wipe it off, treating it like it was dirty, an infection that needed to be cleaned.

The others came out of the truck to greet Mato and congratulate him on a job well done. Mato seemed distressed. He looked at the ganger who was still on the ground. She looked a lot more human with her mask off. She looked normal to him.

"Thank you," the young woman said. Her skin was very dark, just like all the other Scream when they were on the planet. Her eyes were a unique purple and contrasted against her skin. They almost seemed to glow in the dark of the night. 96 moved to the front and signed to her. The Cloud Sister understood and seemed to repeat everything he said by mouthing the words after he signed it. "I don't know where a ship is," she replied.

"That's too bad. If you don't know where a ship is you are not going to very much use to us," Jay stated, pointing his rifle at her. Her eyes went wide, and she moved back. She pushed her body with her hands and feet to get distance a second time. Taryn rushed in the way.

"Stop. I'm not sure how you operate when I'm not around, but this is not going to happen while I am here," exclaimed Taryn.

"A witness is a witness, and we are on the run. We can't afford to be leaving extra people around to give us up."

"There is a better way. I know it."

"Yea probably, but we aren't going to take it," said Jay.

"I'm your boss."

"It isn't worth fighting over." Jay raised his gun back into the air.

A light shone down on them, and the team scrambled. They looked for a place to hide, but there was nowhere to run, not in time before the screeching sounds started. Every single member of the group grabbed their heads. They screamed out and yelled uncontrollably. The sound pierced their skulls, disabling them until they couldn't handle it anymore. They lay on the ground trying to catch their breath. Mato recognized the doctor from before. He could see him from the viewport of the small ship that hovered over them. It was the source of the light and the sound. It was relatively small in ship size. It was about the size of two fighters put together, about fifty meters long. The main access door opened and it lowered itself until it was two meters from the ground. The doctor hopped down then walked in the direction of 96, smiling. 96 could not hear the weapon, so he was immune. He stood there idly while everyone grabbed their heads around him. The doctor came at him lunging, frantically waving and slapping trying to subdue 96 while he dodged the attacks.

Jay was on the ground; the sound disabled his ability to think. He could only roll and yell in agony. His rifle was dropped on the ground in front of him. He pulled on his training. He remembered the wars past and all the near misses that he had survived. He tried to remove his hands from his ears and reach for his weapon. This caused him more pain than he could bear. He was about to pass out from it. The sonic rifle was stationed by Taryn's feet. She screamed and moved her head from side to side. When she was just a second from passing out, the calm wave of no longer being conscious about to comfort her, she was able to see that Jay was grabbing for her feet. She kicked the guns as far as she could under that situation. It didn't help much, but it was just enough to get the clean white straight rifle into his hands.

With a rush of energy, Jay pointed the rifle towards the shuttle and fired. Hitting the interior, the source of the sound, it immediately stopped.

Taryn moved her hands to the front of her, and she could see blood on them. She went into an uncontrolled rage, yelling and hollering. The others stared at her. She looked at the blood and thought about how she had escaped The Scream for so long. How could they have taken away her hearing?

Jay rushed over. "Are you okay?"

"I can't hear anything," she cried. Only the faintest muffle was getting through. She could not make out the words Jay was saying to her as he dropped his rifle and held her while she sat on her knees on the ground.

"You will be okay," said Jay. This time Taryn could make out the words. She continued to sob, but there was relief in sight. Each time Jay said the words she could hear it more and more. Whatever had happened to her was only temporary. *It will be okay*, she told herself.

The rest of the group got up slowly. The doctor signed to Mato, but his helmet did not yet pick it up. Mato touched a button on the side and tried to reboot it thinking that it had been through a lot. *Maybe a reboot will give it some more life.*

The Cloud Sister woke up, and she got on her feet. She put her helmet back on and started to back away so she could get a good view of everyone. She then moved away but picked up her weapon and aimed it at the doctor.

"I should end you for that," the gangster threatened.

Mato's translation helmet kicked back on, and he now could understand what the doctor was signing.

"You owe me," said the translation.

Mato looked up and thought about it.

"Shoot him," said Jay, who was backed up by 96. 96 signed the same thing he obviously wanted the doctor dead. *If it weren't for this doctor, we would all be stuck at the capital under The Magistrate's thumb.*

"You can't be serious," said the Cloud Sister as she moved her gun to face Mato. He raised his sonic pistol and fired. The shot ripped off her shoulder and caused her to pull the trigger by reflex. The shot was wild and did not hit anything, but the doctor smiled.

Galactic Mandate: The Scream

Taryn stood up and wiped her face. "I'm fine. I'm back to normal now. I have had a fear of losing my hearing ever since I was a little girl. But it's ok. It's time to go home. I don't think I can handle much more of this planet. Jay, I really appreciate what you did for me here."

The doctor started signing, and he offered up a pair of keys to the shuttle. "Take my shuttle. It has a zero drive. It's the best money can buy, it even has a cloaking field on it for when I need to visit my more nefarious patients."

"What's in it for you?" asked Jay.

"Nothing. I'm glad I am leaving here with my life. I have too many experiments to run to die now," he replied.

"You know you didn't have a choice about giving up the ship? We were going to take it from you either way," said Jay.

"I've given you the keys. What more do you want?" said the doctor.

Jay gathered his group. He lifted up and carried Taryn to the shuttle. 96 followed suit along with Mato. The doctor stood alone in a field of dead and mangled bodies. He appeared to be waiting, waiting for the right moment to get Mato's attention so he could pull out another device.

The doctor signed to Mato the significance of the device that was in his hand. "Self-Destruct." Mato was looking directly at the doctor. His eyes were fixated. The translation device did its normal job, but it was so damaged that he could barely hear it now. The other members of the crew looked obliviously at the station. Mato pulled the disabling device for this pocket and placed it on 96's back. He quickly ran around so that he could face him. 96 stood with his back to the open shuttle door. "I'm sorry," Mato said hoping his translation helmet could work one more time, then he clicked the trigger. 96 fell backward onto the ground.

The doctor put his trigger back into his pants pocket, and he rushed over to 96. Immediately he started to examine his experiment. He used a small light to test reaction in the eyes, and he put his fingers to 96's neck. A smile could be seen on his face from the shuttle.

Jay didn't react. He saw the entire interaction happen and he went to the pilot's chair, closed the landing door, and engaged the engines. Jay looked over at Mato and waived for him to come to sit by him.

"I was wondering what the real cost of this ship will be. You made a bunch of hard decisions back there," Jay stated.

"I didn't want to kill those people," said Mato.

"I wish I could say neither did I, but I've come to enjoy it now. Killing fuckers. It's just what I am good at, and no one is going to take that away from me without a rifle."

"Does it get easier?" asked Mato.

"No, but it gets funnier," said Jay.

Jay typed in the coordinates to the GPL Headquarters.

The ship ascended in the cloud until it reached orbit.

"Time to go," Jay announced as he initiated the zero drive.

Chapter 18

"I don't need any tricks from the both of you," Mantis announced. He looked towards she who was sitting high in the bleachers above the environmentally controlled dome and the enclosed mud pit fighting ring. The Blood Queen sat there looking down. Her children buzzed about.

"How many children do you have?" Dark Cleo asked of the queen.

"Six. None worthy of replacing me," she replied.

"My boys, they will take command of the military once I retire, like I did for my father."

"Your boys, they are adopted right?" The Blood Queen asked.

"Yes, they are. I'm working on making a daughter the hard way, but I'm not getting any progress with that," said Dark Cleo.

"The hard way is more fun." The queen winked.

Mantis moved close towards the two teenagers that were before him. Variant and Fractal each took a side of the arena and didn't get too close to each other or Mantis.

"He's one of the voices," Variant announced.

"I know. He is one my voices too." Fractal replied.

"Voices. You won't be hearing any voices when I am done with you children," Mantis exclaimed.

The teenagers kicked up dirt as they scurried from side to side in the arena. The armor of Mantis hissed and whistled as he moved. It was no longer the marvel of engineering it once was. Now it was patched together and worked because of the sheer willpower Mantis commanded.

"So, tell me about this peace conference. I hear you, and The Acolytes are reconfirming the peace treaty and setting new terms. You know this can't happen. God-Wrath would have too much time to pay attention to use the Blooden. He still blames us for the last two wars he has lost." The Blood Queen stated.

"Yes, I know. I don't have any intention of keeping the peace. We have been working on something. A surprise for God-Wrath and the others at the Galactic Planetary league. They think that we have been a week without the Keepers and their production facilities, but you know what they say. You shouldn't listen to rumors," said Dark Cleo.

The Blood Queen smiled. She made sure that her children had left her side and turned and looked at Dark Cleo. She placed a soft hand on the top of Cleo's and said. "You know us Queens have to stick together. If you find a way to sabotage this Second Treaty, we will be very grateful. Just like you, we have been planning some surprises for the galaxy. The Blooden are no longer bound to our home planet. My marriage to Mantis has brought me ships and more wealth than I could have imagined."

"A correction of history is in order."

"That it is," The Blood Queen agreed. The queen looked down and waved at her husband. She gave a signal and Mantis headed back towards the entrance of the ring. His head was down, and he looked tired.

"What are you doing?" Cleo asked. Her guards dressed in their normal black uniforms stopped the gladiator from leaving.

"We are getting along so well. I would hate for my husband to ruin it by killing your successors," the queen replied.

"You think that's what was about to happen? Your husband was about to kill my boys? I can see that the Blooden are a bit overconfident," replied Dark Cleo. She turned to the crowd that had gathered and to each gladiator. "The match is still on. Do me proud."

The Blood Queen had a nervous look on her face, and she tried to get Mantis' attention.

"I'll deal with you two after I deal with the children," he threatened the guard.

"Are you sure about this? My empire won't be held responsible for what happens here today?" asked The Blood Queen.

"Don't worry, like I said, we have a surprise for the galaxy and Mantis will be the first to experience it," said Dark Cleo as she sat back down. This time she reached over and put her hand on The

Blood Queen's, trying to comfort the nervous woman. "Enjoy the show."

Chapter 19

The shuttle rocketed out of zero space. It was immediately identified by station command. Jay input his clearance codes. Taryn was sitting at the communications station, talking with her colleagues about her discovery and summarizing what had happened during her time with Dr. Ulises Tom. The scientists on the screen asked if they could see the artifacts and she showed them. Mato had given them to her as a gift during the long ride in zero space to the station. Taryn spoke to them and ordered for the artifacts be locked away in the tombstone once she reached the station.

"These artifacts are too dangerous to left in the hands of the galaxy. We must lock them away. Any tampering with this technology can lead to the galaxy's destruction," warned Taryn.

"Are you sure?" one of the scientists replied.

"I am. Dr. Ulises Tom was getting into some archaic and arcane research from what I can tell, and he was trying to bring something from the unknown to us. Whatever it is, it spells out our doom."

"We will see you when you get here," they replied and cut the line of communication.

League One was a large Space Station that had hundreds of little shuttles going in and out all the time. A small fleet of defense ships circled about. The station shone against the planet from below the mountains Gala. Jay landed the shuttle in the main hanger, next to three large ships obviously designed for research and science.

"Are those yours?" Mato asked.

"Yes, they are. They could be yours as well if you put down the gun and pick up a microscope," she replied.

"No, thanks I don't think that is me," said Mato.

"Suit yourself. Going with Jay is a hard life," she replied.

"It sure is," said Jay. "Can you come with me? I have something to discuss with you in private."

"Sure, let me show you where my apartment is. I'm glad to be home. It's been way too long," said Taryn. She waved her hand and escorted Jay.

"You will be fine without us for a few minutes, right?" Taryn asked of Mato.

"Yes. Didn't you say they have a full cafeteria with free food?"

"We sure do. Not exactly free but you can take whatever you like. It's paid for by the various empires." Taryn replied.

"Sounds free to me," Mato replied as he headed in the other direction.

Taryn moved forward and down the halls. She let Jay follow her to the outer layer of the station and to an elevator that led to the apartment level. They took the elevator to her level, and she waved her hand at her door, which recognized her and opened right away.

"I assume Death's Witness has some accommodations on the station?"

"We have a sales office. Not much, but I can make a cot behind the desk jockeys," said Jay.

"Good," Taryn replied.

"I guess this is it," said Jay.

"Yes, maybe. I don't have any other mission for you. My project is ruined. There is no way I can continue it now. It is too dangerous for the galaxy. The Scream doesn't have the artifacts or Ulises Tom, but I can't give the GPL the power to destroy the galaxy. It's too big of a risk," said Taryn.

"I'm not talking about that. I'm talking about us being on this mission, seeing what you can do in the field. I want you," Jay stated.

"You've made that very clear," she replied.

"Well?"

"If we were to do this, I have conditions. I need commitment. We would have to be married," replied Taryn.

"We are on a space station with nothing but government officials, ministers, and bureaucrats from hell. If you have the documents, something official, it can be arranged," said Jay.

"Are you saying what I think you are saying?" said Taryn

"Yes, will you marry me?" asked Jay.

M.R. Richardson

"YES!" Taryn smiled and hugged Jay locking him in a tight embrace, the tightest she could muster. He went in for a kiss, and they embraced each other lovingly. Taryn could see the stars behind Jay as his back was to the window out into space. She felt at home finally in her apartment. Her fears and thoughts of the current troubles melted away.

Chapter 20

"She has left with all three artifacts."

"*The Kiladon* won't be able to power its main weapon anymore. This is a giant blow for our security, and we will never be able to open the gate without these objects," signed Ismag.

"Then there is only one course of action. Isn't there?" signed The Magistrate.

"A show of strength to hide our weakness," signed Ismag.

"Weakness you sign? No. We are not weak. We have just run out of time. We must play our hand now and leave the rest up to fate. Ever since the doctor appeared at the gate, we have been preparing for this. The last thing the galaxy will hear is our scream as we drag them into the future whether they like it not," signed The Magistrate.

"I'll prepare the fleet," said Ismag.

"Not just the fleet. We will need the entire invasion force for this."

To be continued...

If you like this book, please leave a review online. The only way I can decide whether to commit more time to these characters and this series is by getting feedback from you, the readers. Your opinion matters to me. I have only so much time to craft new stories. Help me invest that time wisely. Plus, reviews are the only way an author can level up and defeat space pirates.

M.R. Richardson

About me

I have roots in California and Washington state. My love for science fiction goes all the way back to the 1990s. I've always wanted to explore new ideas and imagine new concepts. I strive for innovation always and I am glad you decided to take this journey with me. Keep an eye out for me because I love to go to science fiction & fantasy conventions. If you see me there please say hello so we can talk.

www.MR-Richardson.com

www.ingramcontent.com/pod-product-compliance
Lightning Source LLC
Chambersburg PA
CBHW051839170626
46807CB00003B/1259